REIGN OF TERROR

A dazzling collection of macabre tales from the Golden Age of Horror.

Edited by
Michel Parry

Reign of Terror

Great Victorian Horror Stories

 BARNES & NOBLE BOOKS
A DIVISION OF HARPER & ROW, PUBLISHERS
New York, Cambridge, Hagerstown,
Philadelphia, San Francisco, London,
Mexico City, São Paulo, Sydney

First published in Great Britain by Transworld Publishers Ltd. It is here
reprinted by arrangement.

First BARNES & NOBLE BOOKS edition published 1980.

ISBN: 0-06-465106-1

80 81 82 83 84 10 9 8 7 6 5 4 3 2 1

Contents

Acknowledgements

Every effort has been made to ascertain the copyright status of the stories in this collection. In the event of any due acknowledgement being inadvertently omitted, the Editor offers his apologies and expresses his willingness to correct the omission in subsequent editions.

Thanks are due to John Eggling (*Phantasmagoria Books*) and Stanley Nicholls (*Bookends Fantasy Service*) for suggestions and the loan of rare books. And to Martin Walsh for efforts Above and Beyond.

INTRODUCTION

An Age in Horror

> Silently we went round and round,
> And through each hollow mind
> The memory of dreadful things
> Rushed like a dreadful wind,
> And Horror stalked before each man
> And Terror crept behind.

> Oscar Wilde, *The Ballad of Reading Gaol.*

THAT the sixty-four year reign of Queen Victoria generated more than its share of horrors, no one can deny. The backstreets of Victorian London, those grim, overcrowded warrens of despair, were a bustling breeding ground of horror and, if the stories in these pages are to be believed, the evils were not solely confined to the social. It was, after all, amongst those very tenements that the good Doctor Jekyll made the acquaintance of the monstrous Mister Hyde . . . that Count Dracula sought new blood . . . and that the ageless Dorian Gray pursued his quest for novel vices. And, confirming that truth is not only stranger but often more horrifying than fiction, it was in those same joyless streets, where the gaslight glare struggled through an eternal pall of fog thick as the smoke from Stephenson's engines, that there lurked the Demon of Whitechapel, he who sent human kidneys to the police and crowing letters to the press and signed himself, in a red scrawl, *Jack the Ripper.* . . .

Images such as these have impressed upon us a strong association between the Victorian age and things macabre and terrifying. Yet somehow the belief has grown that the actual reign of Victoria produced little of worth in the *genre* of the supernatural and horrific, a misapprehension due largely to the scarcity of surviving material. Fortunately, however, Victorian Supernatural literature is not without its ardent defenders: 'In the ghost story and the tale of terror Victorian authors excelled, and, setting aside the highest masterpieces of literature, there is nothing more difficult to achieve than a first class ghost story.' So wrote the Reverend Montague Summers, an authority on both Supernatural fiction and the Victorians. Summers' bibliographical researches, together with those of his friend S. M. Ellis, have revealed not only the wealth of such fiction produced during the Victorian period but also its crucial importance in the evolution of what has come to be known as the 'horror story'.

At this point, a few words on this term 'horror' are perhaps called for. Some *amateurs* of this kind of literature engage in endless hairsplitting disputes, centred around this word and its close companion 'terror', as to which stories may so be categorised and which may not, and whether or not descriptions such as weird or fantasy or macabre are preferable. The designation 'horror', with its connotations of revulsion, satisfies me no more than it does the purists but I believe that it is the only term which embraces *all* the stories in this collection and which succinctly suggests to the majority of readers what is in store for them. Horror then, in this instance, covers tales of the Supernatural and of physical terror, of ghosts and necromancy and of inhuman violence and all the dark corners and crevices of human belief and behaviour that lie in between.

Throughout the ages, the horrific has fascinated mankind and provided the basis for a recurrent theme in the art and literature of many cultures. For the roots of the modern horror story, however, we need go back no further than to the second half of the eighteenth century. Universally popular at that time were the Gothic novels – lengthy, somewhat incoherent narratives usually set in thunder-shaken mediaeval castles whose labyrinthine passages were, populated by diverse assortments of decadent noblemen, renegade priests, vengeful spectres and fainting ladies. This morbid school of romance, in which the plots often creaked as woefully as the rack in the regulation torture chamber, was accompanied by a revival of interest in the art and architecture of the Middle Ages.

The Gothic novel originated with *The Castle of Otranto* by Horace Walpole, and was extended by writers such as Mrs Radcliffe (*The Mysteries of Udolpho*), Clara Reeve (*The Old English Baron*), William Beckford, the 'Caliph of Fonthill' (*Vathek*), and Matthew Gregory Lewis (*The Monk*, *Legends of Terror*, etc.). The enormous success of these tales of terror, which undoubtedly offered a welcome escape from the straitjacket of Augustan rationalism, led to their being endlessly pirated, plagiarised and, above all, imitated.

The Gothic School captivated the fashionable imagination. Conversation in polite company centred around which was the most shocking work – was it *Horrid Mysteries* or *The Necromancer* or, perhaps, *The Horrors of Oakendale Abbey*? Wealthy noblemen built themselves huge forbidding homes in the Gothic manner and advertised for wild hermits to live in picturesque 'ruins' specially constructed on their estates. The extent to which impressionable young minds (particularly impressionable young *female* minds) were influenced by the crude horrors of the Gothic terror tales has been humorously depicted by Jane Austen in *Northanger Abbey* and Thomas Love Peacock in *Nightmare Abbey*.

Even the abundant real-life blood and terror of the French Revolution did not assuage the taste for the Gothic romances but by the second decade of the nineteenth century, the genre was well in decline. It had been progressively coarsened and cheapened by a flood of lurid, low-priced imitations – the Shilling Shockers and the sixpenny 'blue' books: thirty-six pages of violent thrills bound up with flimsy blue covers bearing the imprint of J. Sabine, B. Crosby, Tegg, Hurst, T. Lowndes, Lemoine, Neil or some other shady publisher.

The Gothic School continued to produce the occasional masterpiece such as *Frankenstein* by Mary Shelley, the teenage wife of the poet, and *Melmoth the Wanderer* by Charles Maturin, but whereas the true Gothics were often grandiose personal visions laden with symbols liberated from the authors subsconscious by dreams, the degenerate imitations were rarely written to satisfy any compulsion other than to make some quick money. Such efforts reduced the terror tale to a repetitive series of shocks loosely strung together by the most convoluted and unconvincing of plots already grown too-familiar to readers sated with the bloodthirsty doings of morbid noblemen and mad monks. The early Gothics had been universally appealing, pleasing master and servant alike, yet discriminating readers held the later caricatures in disdain. As Michael Sadleir, bibliophile author of *Fanny by Gaslight*, put it: 'The Gothic novel crashed and became the vulgar "blood".' One attempt to literally bring new blood to the genre was the steady output during the twenties and thirties of 'Newgate novels', stories of criminals, convicts and murders most foul. The Victorian novelist George Augustus Sala described this development in his autobiographical *Life and Adventures*:

> 'We had done with such ghastly mediaeval romances as Mrs Radcliffe's *Mysteries of Udolpho* and Matthew Lewis' *Monk;* but there had, on the other hand, grown up in the public mind a strange and unwholesome fondness for works of fiction of which criminals of the most flagitious order were the heroes. I cannot help surmising that this morbid partiality was due to the amazingly strong grasp which had been taken of the public curiosity by the revelations incidental to the murder of Weare by Thurtell* and to the forgeries of Fauntleroy the Banker ... Added to the grim notoriety of the two tragedies enacted in the

* William Weare, a gambler, won a considerable amount of money from John Thurtell, a man of enormous build. On October 25th, 1823, Thurtell, together with accomplices Hunt and Probert, lured Weare to a cottage near Elstree where Thurtell was obliged to shoot him, stab him and bash his head in before the terrified victim finally succumbed. One of the stanzas from a broadsheet describing the murder became famous:

> They cut his throat from ear to ear
> His head they battered in.
> His name was Mr William Weare
> He lived in Lyons Inn.

latter years of the reign of George IV must be recalled an unutterably horrible deed of blood perpetrated at Christmas-time, 1837, by one James Greenacre, who murdered and mutilated in a most horrible manner the body of a woman named Hannah Brown.'

Together with the Gothic terror tale, the Newgate Novel was the most important influence on the rapidly evolving school of popular fiction that was to become the staple literary diet of the working class for many years – the 'Penny Dreadful'. Pious Victorians threw their arms up in righteous horror at the obsessive interest inspired by these journals in the fictionalised exploits of Jack Sheppard, Claude Du Val, Dick Turpin and other criminals and highwaymen. Indignant voices warned that such flagrant glamorisation of crime would bring an end to law and order and would swell the ranks of England's criminals to the size of an invincible army. Yet only a few years previously, the same conscientious souls had avidly devoured the picaresque criminal exploits of Bulwer's *Eugene Aram* and *Paul Clifford*, or *Rookwood* by William Harrison Ainsworth.

The Newgate Novel had its run of popularity but held little interest for serious readers and less for serious writers. As early as 1827, Dickens' mentor Leigh Hunt had observed, 'Mere grimness is as easy as grinning; but it requires something to put a handsome face on a story. Narratives become of suspicious merit in proportion as they lean to Newgate-like offenses, particularly of blood and wounds....'

The predictable reaction to the excesses of the Gothic School and its off-shoots took the form of the 'Domestic Story'. Decadent monasteries in Spain and frowning castles atop peaks in the demon-haunted Black Forest were no longer the order of the day. Readers demanded something more closely related to everyday life and the Domestic Story was exactly that. It had no greater aim than to present to the reader middle and upper-class characters in their home environment acting out readily familiar situations. Inevitably, the domestic story made much of manners and morals and undoubtedly contributed to the imposition of the stifling conventions then prevalent.

The Gothic School did not die out entirely. 'The spirit of melodrama and of terror (which is only in rousing guise the spirit of escape) persisted unsubsided and persists to this day,' wrote Michael Sadleir. The persistent influence of the Gothic tales of terror may be found today chiefly in the cinema in the productions of companies such as Hammer Films, in horror comics and, somewhat diluted, in the so-called 'Women's Gothics' – that curiously masochistic brand of literature which chronicles the misadventures of nervous young nurses, invalid companions and governesses lured to remote country houses chockfull of skeleton-brimming cupboards.

The influence of the Domestic Story on the Gothic terror tale was a beneficial steadying one. The Supernatural, which the seance had introduced into fashionable Victorian drawing rooms, was retrieved from distant lands unattainable to the average reader and brought within the bounds of possible experience. The crude extravagant horrors of yesteryear gave way to the subtleties of atmosphere and suggestion and to a nascent grasp of psychology. The child of this union between the Gothic and the Domestic was the Victorian Ghost Story. At its worst this was an insipid colourless creation. At best, it gave rise to masterpieces such as Lord Lytton's *The House and the Brain* and the short stories of Joseph Sheridan Le Fanu.

Obeying the laws of reaction, the pendulum of popular taste swung once more and about the middle of the last century the so-called 'Sensation School' of writers came into prominence. The nucleus of this loosely-categorised group of authors consisted of Dickens, Wilkie Collins, Rhoda Broughton, Ouida, Mary Braddon and Mrs Henry Wood. Initially, these spirited writers received little sympathy from conservative critics who found their realism, not to mention their indecorous inducement to feelings of excitation, abhorrent. But the middle-class public subscribed to their works in vast numbers.

In defining the Sensation Novel a contemporary critic

observed how it was essential that 'it should contain something abnormal and unnatural, something that induces in the simple idea a sort of thrill.' Specialists as they were in stories of mystery and intrigue, the Sensation writers also excelled at supernatural themes and tales of physical terror and are accordingly well represented in the present anthology. The extent of their involvement with such themes may be deduced from a satirical advertisement which appeared in *Punch* in 1863 announcing the publication of a *Sensation Times* devoted to 'Harrowing the Mind, making the Flesh Creep, causing the Hair to stand on End, giving Shocks to the Nervous System, destroying the Conventional Moralities and generally unfitting the Public for the Prosaic Avocations of Life.'

The Sensation writers contributed to the development of what was to become the horror story in a number of ways. They followed the lead of Le Fanu and Poe (who had died prematurely of alcoholism in 1849) in bringing an improved observation of psychology to the characters they depicted. Their characterisations were less stylised and more recognisably human than previously. Plots became more imaginative and yet, at the same time, by virtue of attention to realistic detail, more plausible. Descriptions and dialogue became less high-flown and reflected every-day speech rather than the declamatory language of the Gothic romances.

Not only did the Sensation School exercise a profound effect on the ghost story and tale of terror, but it also helped shape and determine another popular literary form then at the beginning of its evolution – the detective story.

The single most important influence on both *genres* – and on the development of the short story form itself – was the growth of the popular magazines. The favourite fictional medium amongst readers had long been the novel, particularly in three-decker editions, and a writer who envisaged a less macrocosmic endeavour, particularly one whose effectiveness lay in its brevity, had few outlets for a short tale. The usual solution for an author with an idea for a short story was to include it in a novel or serial, under the guise of an anecdote related by some character or other within the larger work. Well-known instances of this device are *Wandering Willie's Tale* from Sir Walter Scott's *Redgauntlet* and the much anthologised 'Werewolf' segment of Frederick Marryat's *The Phantom Ship* (which made its first appearance as a serial in *The New Monthly Magazine* in 1837).

The rise of the fiction-carrying magazines created a reliable market for the short story and encouraged writers to regard the medium in terms of its own merits rather than as an auxiliary form. Of course, some excellent short stories continued to be incorporated into longer works as exemplified in this collection by James Grant's *The Phantom Regiment*, *The Signalman* by Dickens and *The Dream Woman* by Wilkie Collins. Derived from the novel was the device, frequently employed in early ghost stories including *The Monk's Story* by Mrs Crowe, of introducing the reader to a narrator who tells the story proper. Doubtless this imparted a touch of authenticity to the subsequent narrative and helped dispel any doubts that the reader might harbour as to the truth of the tale.

The influential magazines of the Victorian age were many. *Chamber's Journal*, *The Argosy*, *Temple Bar*, *Pall Mall*, *Belgravia*, *Household Words*, *All the Year Round*, *Reynold's Miscellany*, *Bentley's Miscellany*, *The Cornhill*, *Cassell's*, *The Strand* – these are but a few of the titles which flourished. It was in such magazines as these that many of the stories I have collected together first appeared and details of their background and circulations help us appreciate how widespread was the taste for fiction of this kind and who the original readers were. *Blackwood's Edinburgh Magazine*, from which I have selected several stories, amongst them *Horror: a True Tale*, was established in 1817 in opposition to *The Edinburgh Review*. Affectionately known as 'Maga' to its predominantly Tory readership, *Blackwood's* was priced at half-a-crown, no trifling sum in those days. Such an elevated price ensured that it was delivered only to the country mansions and town houses of Britain's most privileged citizens. Not surprisingly,

* See *The 2nd Corgi Book of Great Victorian Horror Stories*.

records show that its circulation in 1831 was only 8,000. In contrast, the average circulation of *Household Words*, a much livelier publication under the editorship of Dickens, was 40,000, most of the readers belonging to the lower middle class. The first issue of its successor, *All the Year Round*, which was owned as well as edited by Dickens, sold 120,000 copies and when Dickens serialised one of his phenomenally popular novels, the readership soared to as many as 300,000. Considering that stories of ghosts and other terrors appeared not infrequently in both *Blackwood's* and *All the Year Round* as well as those magazines which bridged the broad diversity of taste between them, it becomes apparent that the appeal of such fare transcended class barriers as could no other form of literature. Naturally, it would be wrong to suggest that these stories found favour with *everybody*. There was undoubtedly a sizeable section of the community who, as Richard Altick put it in *The English Common Reader*, affected an 'evangelical horror of imaginative indulgence'. It is not, perhaps, too indulgent to imagine that it was devout persons such as these, with their emphasis on devotional literature and 'improving facts', who forced upon their children those grim moralising Victorian fairy tales, the cautionary cruelties of which now seem to us more horrifying than the harmless fantasies which their advocates decried.*

Christmas, as Dickens has shown us, was an event which the Victorians knew well how to celebrate and a favourite Christmas Eve entertainment was the telling of scalp-tingling stories round the cheery hearth. The Christmas issues of many magazines entered into the festive mood by carrying a seasonal ghost story or two – or even a whole issue's worth – and in this way some of our finest ghost stories have come to us. In the same spirit were the special Christmas Annuals, sometimes wholly taken up by a book-length ghost tale. *The Haunted River* by Mrs J. H. Riddell (whose absence from this anthology I very much regret) comprised the whole of

---

* *Under the Sunset*, Bram Stoker's comparatively mild collection of allegorical stories for children, dealt with such pleasantries as spectral plagues, bleeding giants and a grim King of Death.

Routledge's Christmas Annual for 1877 and the following year *Routledge's* offered the same author's *Disappearance of Mr Jeriamiah Redworth*.

Ghosts, whether fictional or factual, held an obsessive interest for the Victorians – an interest which was given considerable impetus in 1848 by the publication of a bulky two-volume work described as the 'most compendious collection of ghost-stories in the language': *The Night Side of Nature* by Mrs Catherine Crowe. In this book, Mrs Crowe, who had previously been better known as a writer of domestic novels such as *Susan Hopley* and *Lilly Dawson* than as a propagandist for belief in ghosts, collected together hundreds of allegedly true accounts of spirits and hauntings. Despite a defensive introduction, the book's sincerity and cumulative impact still holds considerable persuasive power. Mrs Crowe's later books on the Supernatural, *Ghosts and Family Legends*, *Stories of Light and Darkness* and *Spiritualism and the Age We Live In* met with a success equal to her first. In 1850, Dom Augustine Calmet's classic work of 1749, *Dissertation sur les Apparitions des Esprits et sur les Vampires et Revenants*, was rendered into English as *The Phantom World*. Its authentic eyewitness accounts of blood-gorged Vampires and other supernatural horrors lent further weight to belief in the restlessness of the dead (and influenced the writing of Le Fanu's novelette *Carmilla* and, thereby indirectly, Bram Stoker's *Dracula*).

The Victorian interest in ghosts and related phenomena was no short-lived fad. In 1891, more than forty years after the publication of *The Night Side of Nature*, a similar work entitled *Real Ghost Stories** sold over a hundred thousand copies in one week and went into several subsequent editions. Together with the popularity of spooks came Spiritualism and all its attendant paraphernalia of table-rapping, trance mediums, ouija boards, disembodied hands and Red Indian

* *Real Ghost Stories* carried the following thoughtful Caution to the reader: 'Please Note that the narratives printed in these pages had better not be read by any one of tender years, of morbid excitability or of excessively nervous temperament.'

spirit guides. There was no lack of charlatans but there were some truly remarkable cases such as that of Daniel Dunglas Home, the Scottish medium who had a disconcerting tendency to float out of rooms through one window and back in again through another. Home was a frequent guest at Knebworth, home of Edward Bulwer Lytton, himself a keen student of the occult and author of *The House and the Brain*.

Why were the Victorians so fascinated by ghosts? Such a question may never now be satisfactorily answered but undoubtedly it was to a large extent due to a reaction against rigid disbelief in the Age of Reason when even fictional ghosts were unmasked as human agencies in the final chapter. Wrote Mrs Crowe: 'the contemptuous scepticism of the last age is yielding to a more humble spirit of enquiry; and there is a large class of persons amongst the most enlightened of the present who are beginning to believe that much which they have been taught to reject as fable, has been, in reality, ill-understood truth.' This relaxation of prejudice towards the supernatural must have been influenced by the impact at home of travellers' tales of strange sights in the colonies.

Perhaps the essayist William Roscoe came even closer to answering when, in a review of *The Night Side of Nature*, he observed, 'You cannot subject a ghost to scientific scrutiny under a microscope, or otherwise.' Belief in ghosts was distinctly reassuring in an age of crass materialism, one in which the tearaway infant prodigy Science seemed ready, at times, to discard entirely its old nanny, the Church. Ghosts, if they existed, were evidence of a spiritual world beyond the reach of the probing, dissecting fingers of scientists, to say nothing of confirmation of one of the Church's principal tenets – Life after Death. And, then as now, ghosts had the unique advantage of being exceedingly difficult to prove or disprove. The question, 'Are there such things as ghosts?' could be answered with as much assurance and authority by the merest Street Arab as by a member of the Royal Society or the Archbishop of Canterbury.

No doubt fully aware of the irresolveable nature of the

problem, scientists chose to ignore the matter of ghosts. Both Mrs Crowe and William Stead*, author of *Real Ghost Stories*, took them to task for this unscientific attitude. 'The Inquisitor who forbade free inquiry into matters of religion because of human depravity,' wrote Stead, 'was the natural precursor of the Scientist who forbids the exercise of reason on the subject of ghosts, on account of inherited tendencies to attribute such phenomenon outside the established order of nature.' It is significant that whilst Mrs Crowe showed a certain satisfaction at the exclusion of ghosts from the apparently inviolable order of nature, Stead, writing at a time when further inroads had been made into psychology, and the soul had tentatively been identified as the Unconscious Personality, resented this exclusion: 'Those who treat them with this injustice,' he wryly observed, 'need not wonder if they take their revenge in "creeps".'

This brief survey of horror fiction in the reign of Victoria would not be complete without a few words on what Wilkie Collins, writing in *Household Words*, described as 'the mysterious, the unfathomable, the universal public of the penny-novel journals.' This section of the reading community, so puzzling to middle-class observers, comprised the literate and semi-literate members of the working class – the domestic servants, apprentices, factory workers and labourers. Like those better-favoured than themselves, this group had a pronounced taste for the macabre but preferred it laced with a good strong dose of blood and sensationalism. In the early years of the reign, this appetite was still catered for by the 'running patterers' or broadsheet peddlers. The patterers moved quickly from street to street advertising in stentorian fashion the exciting qualities and desirability of their broadsheets which most likely came from the notorious district of Seven Dials where James Catnach, the most successful of broadsheet publishers, had his presses. They

* A newspaper editor, Stead achieved considerable notoriety (and a brief term of imprisonment) by *buying* outright a thirteen-year-old English girl to lend weight to his crusading campaign against child prostitution and the white slave traffic in Europe.

might have been traditional favourites – jokes and nursery rhymes – or else dealt with some political scandal of the day; but the bestselling broadsheets of all were concerned with details of topical murders and executions. A good imaginative murder sold hundreds of thousands of broadsheets to be eagerly read aloud in crowded pubs or around the dinner table. Murderers' confessions were an especially reliable moneyspinner for Catnach and his rivals, though many a condemned man would have been surprised to read the passionate words of repentance attributed him by some Grub Street hack. *The Confession and Execution of William Corder*, the celebrated 'Red Barn' murderer, reputedly sold over three quarters of a million copies. And the number of broadsheets sold dealing with the execution of James Greenacre and his lover Sarah Gale for the murder (Sala's 'unutterably horrible deed of blood') of Hannah Brown in 1837 totalled a staggering 1,650,000.

Broadsheets describing executions were written and printed ahead of the event so as to catch the high tide of public interest. Consequently, in the rare instances of a reprieve, the patterer had plenty of explaining to do when news of the pardon reached the district where he was busily hawking broadsheets describing the condemned man's death agonies!

There existed a more humorous type of broadsheet known as a 'cock'. Cocks usually recounted some astonishingly unlikely occurrence purported to have happened to a local person and invariably they climaxed with a pathetic twist. A popular cock entitled *An Account of the Dreadful Apparition that appeared last Night to Henry – in this street, of Mary – the shopkeeper's daughter round the corner, in a shroud, all covered in white* shows how much a part of popular culture the Supernatural had become in the early years of Victoria's reign – he ventured for a moment to raise his eyes; when – my blood freezes as I relate it – before him stood the figure of Mary in a shroud – her beamless eyes fixed upon him with a vacant stare, and her bared bosom exposing a most deadly gash.

'Henry, Henry, Henry!' she repeated in a hollow tone –
'Henry! I am come for thee! Thou hast often said that
death with me was preferable to life without me; Come
then, and enjoy with me all the ecstasies of love these
ghastly features, added to the contemplation of a charnel
house, can inspire'

As I touched upon previously, the Gothic novel was
superseded by its bastard offspring, the Shilling Shocker.
This, in turn, gave way to the Penny Dreadful, which
remained the principal means of dispensing thrills, fantasy
and horror to the working classes throughout almost the
whole of the Victorian age. The true progenitor of the Penny
Dreadfuls, or 'Bloods' as they were sometimes called, was the
low-priced chapbook which offered a condensed version of
The Monk or some other infamous Gothic novel, retaining
only the most awesome and harrowing highlights. The
popularity of these digests made the appearance of regular
periodicals devoted to such fare inevitable. Significantly,
the first publication to be issued in weekly serial parts of
which we have record made its appearance in 1826 under
the title of *Legends of Terror, and Tales of the Wonderful and
Wild.*

The pattern of publication of the Penny Dreadfuls was
quickly and profitably established. Once a suitably alluring
title had been decided on, the publisher set to work on it one
of his familiar hacks, usually at the rate of ten shillings an
issue. Plots, improvised as the author wrote, grew with all
the ingenuity and resilience of a house of cards. If a title did
not inflame the popular imagination and sell a satisfactory
number of issues, the writer would be instructed to serve
up a bonus of blood and thunderous horror in the next
instalment. Should this device fail, the tale might be quickly
concluded and dropped in favour of a new and more promising title. Otherwise stories were extended as long as the
demand (and the author's inventiveness) persevered, this
being anything between twenty and two hundred issues.

Bloods such as *The Haunted House, or, Love and Crime*;

Joskin the Bodysnatcher; *The Horrors of the Haunted Cellar*; *The Vampire Demon* and *The Skeleton Horseman, or, the Shadow of Death* were bought in their thousands from the 'tobacconist and sweetstuff vender and the keeper of the small chandlery.' Their success was enormous, lasting, and, naturally, not without considerable outraged criticism from the self-appointed moral watchdogs of the nation. 'Upwards of a million of these weekly pen'orths of abomination find customers,' lamented James Greenwood in his voyeuristic *Wilds of London* published in 1876. Christian philanthropic organisations such as the Society for the Diffusion of Useful Knowledge tried to woo working class readers from the Bloods with penny magazines of a wholesome and uplifting kind but the masses stuck resolutely to more appetising titles like *Secrets of the Sewers of London* and *Secrets of the Dissecting Room*. It is interesting to speculate on why, when the middle classes liked their ghosts to be British and haunt at home, the Penny Dreadfuls followed the Gothic tradition in situating many of their terrors abroad. Possibly slum dwellers found it easier to return to reality after reading of the disadvantages of living in a stately *château* in the horror-haunted wilds of the Black Forest or Hartz Mountains.

The horrors resident there were nothing compared to the horror with which the middle classes viewed the literature of the streets. Probably this was not so much a manifestation of concern for what was being read below stairs as of fear that the clean unsullied minds of *their own* would be contaminated. Certainly it was not unknown for enterprising middle class youths, Charles Dickens, Robert Louis Stevenson and G. K. Chesterton amongst them, to secretly collect the rip-roaring shockers of which their elders so disapproved.

That seditious bogeyman, the author of Penny Dreadfuls, seems to have occupied the same place in contemporary bourgeois fears as the drug-dealing Communist agitator today. Warned James Greenwood:

'Beware of him, O careful parents of little lads! He is as cunning as the fabled Vampire. Already he may have bitten your little rosy-cheeked son Jack. He may be lurking at this very moment in that young gentleman's private chamber, little as you suspect it, polluting his mind and smoothing the way that leads to swift destruction.'

The most prolific of these Vampires was Thomas Peskett Prest who, appropriately, is credited with authorship of one of the most notorious of the Penny Dreadfuls, *Varney the Vampire, or, The Feast of Blood.* Other characteristic titles of this author's output are *The Maniac Father, or, The Victim of Seduction; The Death Grasp, or, a Father's Curse; Almira's Curse, or, The Black Tower of Brandsdorf; The Skeleton Clutch, or, the Goblet of Gore; and The Death Ship, or, the Pirate's Bride and the Maniac of the Deep.* Prest wrote chiefly for Edward Lloyd who, like many rival publishers of street literature, kept his offices in Salisbury Square near Fleet Street. Throughout the 1840's Lloyd published about two hundred Penny Dreadfuls, half of which were written by the indomitable Prest. At the time of his death, Lloyd was a newspaper magnate of considerable importance and left half a million pounds. Obituaries tastefully avoided mentioning his dark and dreadful past as a publisher of penny fiction.

The popularity of the Bloods declined with the spread of penny journals offering a wider choice of fiction and articles, and three or four times the amount for the same price. By 1890 sales had greatly fallen off but old favourites were still available in single aggregate volumes priced sixpence.

Towards the end of the century, writers working in a loftier area of literature such as Rudyard Kipling, Thomas Hardy and Joseph Conrad had dabbled with tales of horror and the supernatural. Arthur Conan Doyle, later to be a staunch supporter of Spiritualism, penned some powerful, pre-Holmesian ghost stories and the advent of H. G. Wells firmly extended the terror tale into the domain of Science. As the Victorian era drew to a close, such future masters of horror as Arthur Machen, Robert Hichens, M. P. Shiel and F. Marion Crawford were seeing their first works published.

And, as I mentioned in opening, it was the Victorian age that gave us three immortal classics of terror: Oscar Wilde's *The Portrait of Dorian Gray* (1884), Robert Louis Stevenson's *Doctor Jekyll and Mister Hyde* (1886) and Bram Stoker's *Dracula* (1897). Truly then, a Reign of Terror!

If this collection helps in some way vindicate Victorian supernatural and horror fiction and return it to its rightful position of pre-eminence, I shall be well pleased. But, to be honest, my principal aim in compiling these stories is somewhat more modest. Like Dickens' Fat Boy, 'I only *wants to make your flesh creep.* . . .'

Michel Parry

A Singular Passage in the Life of the Late Henry Harris, Doctor in Divinity

As related by the Rev. Jasper Ingoldsby, M.A., his friend and executor

The Ingoldsby Legends, *the collection of grotesque, fantastic narratives in prose and verse, from which this story is taken, hold a unique position in English Literature – perhaps analogous to that of Balzac's* Contes Drolatiques *in French Literature. Certainly no work of macabre fantasy has ever been so enthusiastically received by critics and the reading public alike as was* The Ingoldsby Legends.

Attributed to one Jasper Ingoldsby, these bizarre but often amusing creations were actually the work of Richard Harris Barham (1788– 1845), a clergyman who was once Minor Canon of St Paul's in London. A lively extrovert, Barham was no stranger to London literary circles and counted amongst his close friends the historical romanticist William Harrison Ainsworth, a fellow exponent of the later Gothic tradition. Barham started his literary career in 1819 when, being laid up in bed for a few weeks after a coaching accident, he spent his time writing a novel, Baldwin. *Thereafter, he contributed many essays, reviews and poems to fashionable magazines but found little time to undertake anything lengthier. The first of the* Legends *appeared in 1826 but it was not until 1836 that Barham's old schoolfriend Richard Bentley, a publisher, commissioned him to write a regular series for his magazine* Bentley's Miscellany, *then being skilfully edited by a young man named Charles Dickens. The series was an immediate success and in 1840* The Ingoldsby Legends *first appeared in book form.*

Barham never considered his teralary activities to be very much more than a hobby and he once commented, 'Give me a story to tell and I can tell it in my own way; but I can't invent one.' Although this statement is undoubtedly over-modest, most of the Legends *were based on authentic legends and folk-traditions Barham picked up around the country or which were told to him by a Mrs Hughes, a literary enthusiast who had helped him get his earlier work published (she was also the grandmother of Tom Hughes who wrote* Tom Brown's Schooldays.)

Whilst Barham's novels and other writings have fallen into complete obscurity, The Ingoldsby Legends *are sure to go on entertaining – and frightening – readers for many years to come.*

IN order that the extraordinary circumstance which I am about to relate may meet with the credit it deserves, I think it necessary to promise, that my reverend friend, among whose papers I find it recorded, was in his lifetime ever esteemed as a man of good plain understanding, strict veracity, and unimpeached morals, – by no means of a nervous temperament, or one likely to attach undue weight to any occurrence out of the common course of events, merely because his reflections might not, at the moment, afford him a ready solution of its difficulties.

On the truth of his narrative, as far as he was personally concerned, no one who knew him would hesitate to place the most implicit reliance. His history is briefly this: He had married early in life and was a widower at the age of thirty-nine, with an only daughter, who had then arrived at puberty, and was just married to a near connection of our own family. The sudden death of her husband, occasioned by a fall from his horse, only three days after her confinement, was abruptly communicated to Mrs S— by a thoughtless girl, who saw her master brought lifeless into the house, and, with all that inexplicable anxiety to be the first to tell bad news, so common among the lower orders, rushed at once into the sick-room with her intelligence. The shock was too severe: and though the young widow survived the fatal event several months, yet she gradually sank under the blow, and expired leaving a boy, not a twelvemonth old, to the care of his maternal grandfather.

My poor friend was sadly shaken by this melancholy catastrophe; time, however, and a strong religious feeling, succeeded at length in moderating the poignancy of his grief – a consummation much advanced by his infant charge, who now succeeded, as it were by inheritance, to the place in his affections left vacant by his daughter's demise. Frederick S— grew up to be a fine lad, his personal features were decidedly handsome; still there was, as I remember, an unpleasant expression in his countenance, and an air of reserve, attributed, by the few persons who called occasionally at the vicarage, to the retired life led by his grandfather, and the little opportunity he had, in consequence, of mixing in the society of his equals in age and intellect. Brought up entirely at home, his progress in the common branches of education was, without any great display of precocity, rather in advance of the generality of boys of his own standing; partly owing, perhaps, to the turn which even his amusements took from the first. His sole associate was the son of the village apothecary, a boy about two years older than himself, whose father being really clever in his profession, and a good operative chemist, had constructed for himself a small laboratory, in which, as he was fond of children, the two boys spent a great portion of their leisure time, witnessing many of those little experiments so attractive to youth, and in time aspiring to imitate what they admired.

In such society, it is not surprising that Frederick S— should imbibe a strong taste for the sciences which formed his principal amusement; or that, when, in process of time, it became necessary to choose his walk in life, a profession so intimately connected with his favourite pursuit as that of medicine should be eagerly selected. No opposition was offered by my friend, who knowing that the greater part of his own income would expire with his life, and that the remainder would prove an insufficient resource to his grandchild, was only anxious that he should follow such a path as would secure him that moderate and respectable competency which is, perhaps, more conducive to real happiness than a more elevated or wealthy station. Frederick was, accordingly, at the proper age, matriculated at Oxford, with the view of studying the higher branches of medicine, a few months after his friend, John W—, had proceeded to Leyden, for the purpose of making himself acquainted with the practice of surgery in the hospitals and lecture-rooms attached to that university. The boyish intimacy of their younger days did not, as is frequently the case, yield to separation; on the contrary, a close correspondence was kept up between them. Dr Harris was even prevailed upon to allow Frederick to take a trip to Holland to see his friend: and John returned the visit to Frederick at Oxford.

Satisfactory as, for some time, were the accounts of the general course of Frederick S—'s studies, by degrees rumours of a less pleasant nature reached the ears of some of his friends; to the vicarage, however, I have reason to believe they never penetrated. The good old Doctor was too well beloved in his parish for any one voluntarily to give him pain; and, after all, nothing beyond whispers and surmises had reached X—, when the worthy vicar was surprised on a sudden by a request from his grandchild, that he might be permitted to take his name off the books of the university, and proceed to finish his education in conjunction with his friend W— at Leyden. Such a proposal, made, too, at a time when the period for his graduating could not be far distant, both surprised and grieved the Doctor; he combated the design with more perseverance than he had ever been known to exert in opposition to any declared wish of his darling boy before, but, as usual, gave way, when, more strongly pressed, from sheer inability to persist in a refusal which seemed to give so much pain to Frederick, especially when the latter, with more energy than was quite becoming their relative situations, expressed his positive determination of not returning to Oxford, whatever might be the result of his grandfather's decision. My friend, his mind, perhaps, a little weakened by a short but severe nervous attack from which he had scarcely recovered, at length yielded a reluctant consent, and Frederick quitted England.

It was not till some months had elapsed after his departure, that I had reason to suspect that the eager desire of availing himself of opportunities for study abroad, not afforded him at home, was not the sole, or even the principal, reason which had drawn Frederick so abruptly from his *Alma Mater*. A chance visit to the university, and a conversation with a senior fellow belonging to his late college, convinced me of this; still I found it impossible to extract from the latter the precise nature of his offence. That he had given way to most culpable indulgences I had before heard hinted; and when I recollected how he had been at once launched, from a state of what might be well called seclusion, into a world where so many enticements were lying in wait to allure – with liberty, example, everything to tempt him from the straight road – regret, I frankly own, was more the predominant feeling in my mind than either surprise or condemnation. But there was evidently something more than mere ordinary excess – some act of profligacy, perhaps of a deeper stain, which had induced his superior, who, at first, had been loud in his praises, to desire him to withdraw himself quietly, but for ever; and such an intimation, I found, had, in fact, been conveyed to him from an authority which it was impossible to resist. Seeing that my informant was determined not to be explicit, I did not press for a disclosure, which, if made, would, in all probability, only have given me pain, and that the rather, as my old friend the Doctor had recently obtained a valuable living from Lord M—, only a few miles distant from the market town in which I resided, where he now was, amusing himself in putting his grounds into order, ornamenting his house, and getting everything ready against his grandson's expected visit in the following autumn. October came, and with it came Frederick; he rode over more than once to see me, sometimes accompanied by the Doctor, between whom and myself the recent loss of my poor daughter Louisa had drawn the cords of sympathy still closer.

More than two years had flown on in this way, in which Frederick S— had as many times made temporary visits to his native country. The time was fast approaching when he was expected to return and finally take up his residence in England, when the sudden illness of my wife's father obliged us to take a journey into Lancashire; my old friend, who had himself a curate, kindly offered to fix his quarters at my parsonage, and superintend the concerns of my parish till my return. Alas! when I saw him next he was on the bed of death!

My absence was necessarily prolonged much beyond what I had anticipated. A letter, with a foreign post-mark, had, as I afterwards found, been brought over from his house to my venerable substitute in the interval, and barely giving himself time to transfer the charge he had undertaken to a neighbouring clergyman, he had hurried off at once to Leyden. His arrival there was however too late. Frederick *was dead!* – killed in a duel, occasioned, it was said, by no ordinary provocation on his part, although the flight of his antagonist had added to the mystery which enveloped his origin. The long journey, its melancholy termination, and the complete overthrow of all my poor friend's earthly hopes, were too much for him. He appeared too – as I was informed by the proprietor of the house in which I found him, when his summons at length had brought me to his bedside – to have received some sudden and unaccountable shock, which even the death of his grandson was inadeqate to explain. There was, indeed, a wildness in his fast-glazing eye, which mingled strangely with the glance of satisfaction thrown upon me as he pressed my hand; he endeavoured to raise himself, and would have spoken, but fell back in the effort, and closed his eyes for ever. I buried him there, by the side of the object of his more than parental affection – in a foreign land.

It is from papers that I discovered in his travelling case that I submit the following extracts, without, however, presuming to advance an opinion on the strange circumstances which they detail, or even as to the connection which some may fancy they discover between different parts of them.

The first was evidently written at my own house, and bears date August the 15th, 18—, about three weeks after my own departure for Preston.

It begins thus:—

'Tuesday, August 15. – Poor girl! – I forget who it is that says, "The real ills of life are light in comparison with fancied evils"; and certainly the scene I have just witnessed goes some way towards establishing the truth of the hypothesis. Among the afflictions which flesh is heir to, a diseased imagination is far from being the lightest, even when considered separately, and without taking into the account those bodily pains and sufferings which – so close is the connection between mind and matter – are but too frequently attendant upon any disorder of the fancy. Seldom has my interest been more powerfully excited than by poor Mary Graham. Her age, her appearance, her pale, melancholy features, the very contour of her countenance, all conspire to remind me, but too forcibly, of one who, waking or sleeping, is never long absent from my thoughts; – but enough of this.

'A fine morning had succeeded one of the most tempestuous nights I ever remember, and I was just sitting down to a substantial breakfast, which the care of my friend Ingoldsby's housekeeper, kind-hearted Mrs Wilson, had prepared for me, when I was interrupted by a summons to the sickbed of a young parishioner whom I had frequently seen in my walks, and had remarked for the regularity of her attendance at Divine worship. Mary Graham is the elder of two daughters, residing with their mother, the widow of an attorney, who, dying suddenly in the prime of life, left his family but slenderly provided for. A strict though not parsimonious economy has, however, enabled them to live with an appearance of respectability and comfort; and from the personal attractions which both the girls possess, their mother is evidently not without hopes of seeing one, at least, of them advantageously settled in life. As far as poor Mary is concerned, I fear she is doomed to inevitable disappointment, as I am much mistaken if consumption has not laid its wasting finger upon her; while this last recurrence, of what

33

I cannot but believe to be a formidable epileptic attack, threatens to shake out, with even added velocity, the little sand that may yet remain within the hour-glass of time. Her very delusion, too, is of such a nature as, by adding to bodily illness the agitation of superstitious terror, can scarcely fail to accelerate the catastrophe, which I think I see fast approaching.

'Before I was introduced into the sickroom, her sister, who had been watching my arrival from the window, took me into their little parlour, and, after the usual civilities, began to prepare me for the visit I was about to pay. Her countenance was marked at once with trouble and alarm, and in a low tone of voice, which some internal emotion, rather than the fear of disturbing the invalid in a distant room, had subdued almost to a whisper, informed me that my presence was become necessary, not more as a clergyman than a magistrate; that the disorder with which her sister had, during the night, been so suddenly and unaccountably seized, was one of no common kind, but attended with circumstances which, coupled with the declarations of the sufferer, took it out of all ordinary calculations, and, to use her own expression, that, "malice was at the bottom of it".

'Naturally supposing that these insinuations were intended to intimate the partaking of some deleterious substance on the part of the invalid, I inquired what reason she had for imagining, in the first place, that anything of a poisonous nature had been administered at all; and, secondly, what possible incitement any human being could have for the perpetration of so foul a deed towards so innocent and un-offending an individual? Her answer considerably relieved the apprehensions I had begun to entertain lest the poor girl should, from some unknown cause, have herself been attempting to rush uncalled into the presence of her Creator; at the same time, it surprised me not a little by its apparent want of rationality and common-sense. She had no reason to believe, she said, that her sister had taken poison, or that any attempt upon her life had been made, or was, perhaps, contemplated, but that "still malice was at work – the malice of villains or fiends, or of both combined; that no causes purely natural would suffice to account for the state in which her sister had been now twice placed, or for the dreadful sufferings she had undergone while in that state"; and that she was determined the whole affair should undergo a thorough investigation. Seeing that the poor girl was now herself labouring under a great degree of excitement, I did not think it necessary to enter at that moment into a discussion upon the absurdity of her opinion, but applied myself to the tranquillising of her mind by assurances of a proper inquiry, and then drew her attention to the symptoms of the indisposition, and the way in which it had first made its appearance.

'The violence of the storm last night had, I found, induced the whole family to sit up far beyond their usual hour, till, wearied out at length, and, as their mother observed, "tired of burning fire and candle to no purpose," they repaired to their several chambers.

'The sisters occupied the same room; Elizabeth was already at her humble toilet, and had commenced the arrangement of her hair for the night, when her attention was at once drawn from her employment by a half-smothered shriek and exclamation from her sister, who, in her delicate state of health, had found walking up two flights of stairs, perhaps a little more quickly than usual, an exertion, to recover from which she had seated herself in a large arm-chair.

'Turning hastily at the sound, she perceived Mary deadly pale, grasping, as it were convulsively, each arm of the chair which supported her, and bending forward in the attitude of listening; her lips were trembling and bloodless, cold drops of perspiration stood upon her forehead, and in an instant after, exclaiming in a piercing tone, "Hark! they are calling me again! it is – *it is the same voice*; – Oh no, no! – O my God! save me, Betsy – hold me – save me!" she fell forward upon the floor. Elizabeth flew to her assistance, raised her, and by her cries brought both her mother, who had not yet got into bed, and their only servant-girl, to her aid. The latter was despatched at once for medical help; but, from the appearance of the sufferer, it was much to be feared that she would soon be beyond the reach of art. Her agonised parent and sister succeeded in bearing her between them and placing her on a bed: a faint and intermittent pulsation was for a while perceptible; but in a few moments a general shudder shook the whole body; the pulse ceased, the eyes became fixed and glassy, the jaw dropped, a cold clamminess usurped the place of the genial warmth of life. Before Mr I— arrived everything announced that dissolution had taken place, and that the freed spirit had quitted its mortal tenement.

'The appearance of the surgeon confirmed their worst apprehensions; a vein was opened, but the blood refused to flow, and Mr I— pronounced that the vital spark was indeed extinguished.

'The poor mother, whose attachment to her children was perhaps the most powerful, as they were the sole relatives or connections she had in the world, was overwhelmed with a grief amounting almost to frenzy; it was with difficulty that she was removed to her own room by the united strength of her daughter and medical adviser. Nearly an hour had elapsed during the endeavour at calming her transports; they had succeeded, however, to a certain extent, and Mr I— had taken his leave, when Elizabeth, re-entering the bedchamber in which her sister lay, in order to pay the last sad duties to her corpse, was horrorstruck at seeing a crimson stream of blood running down the side of the counterpane to the floor. Her exclamation brought the girl again to her side, when it was perceived, to their astonishment, that the sanguine stream proceeded from the arm of the body, which was now manifesting signs of returning life. The half-frantic mother flew to the room, and it was with difficulty that they could prevent her, in her agitation, from so acting as to extinguish for ever the hope which had begun to rise in their bosoms. A long-drawn sigh, amounting almost to a groan, followed by several convulsive gaspings, was the prelude in the restoration of the animal functions in poor Mary: a shriek, almost preternaturally loud, considering her state of exhaustion, succeeded; but she did recover, and, with the help of restoratives, was well enough towards morning to express a strong desire that I should be sent for – a desire the more readily complied with, inasmuch as the strange expressions and declarations she had made since her restoration to consciousness, had filled her sister with the most horrible suspicions. The nature of these suspicions was such as would at any other time, perhaps, have raised a smile upon my lips; but the distress, and even agony of the poor girl, as she half hinted and half expressed them, were such as entirely to preclude every sensation at all approaching to mirth. Without endeavouring, therefore, to combat ideas, evidently too strongly impressed upon her mind at the moment to admit of present refutation, I merely used a few encouraging words, and requested her to precede me to the sick-chamber.

'The invalid was lying on the outside of the bed, partly dressed, and wearing a white dimity wrapping gown, the colour of which corresponded but too well with the deadly paleness of her complexion. Her cheek was wan and sunken, giving an extraordinary prominence to her eye, which gleamed with a lustrous brilliancy not unfrequently characteristic of the aberration of intellect. I took her hand; it was chill and clammy, the pulse feeble and intermittent, and the general debility of her frame was such that I would fain have persuaded her to defer any conversation which, in her present state, she might not be equal to support. Her positive assurance that, until she had disburdened herself of what she called her "dreadful secret", she could know no rest either of mind or body, at length induced me to comply with her wish, opposition to which, in her then frame of mind, might perhaps be attended with even worse effects than its indulgence. I bowed acquiescence, and in a low and faltering voice, with frequent interruptions, occasioned by her weakness, she gave me the following singular account of the sensations which, she averred, had been experienced by her during her trance:

' "This, sir," she began, "is not the first time that the cruelty of others has, for what purpose I am unable to conjecture, put me to a degree of torture which I can compare to no suffering, either of body or mind, which I have ever before experienced. On a former occasion I was willing to believe it the mere effect of a hideous dream, or what is vulgarly termed the nightmare; but this repetition, and the circumstances under which I was last *summoned*, at a time, too, when I had not even composed myself to rest, fatally convince me of the reality of what I have seen and suffered.

' "This is no time for concealment of any kind. It is now more than a twelvemonth since I was in the habit of occasionally encountering in my walks a young man of prepossessing appearance and gentlemanly deportment. He was always alone, and generally reading; but I could not be long in doubt that these re-encounters, which became every week more frequent, were not the effect of accident, or that his attention, when we did meet, was less directed to his book than to my sister and myself. He even seemed to wish to address us, and I have no doubt would have taken some other opportunity of doing so, had not one been afforded him by a strange dog attacking us one Sunday morning on our way to church, which he beat off, and made use of this little service to promote an acquaintance. His name, he said, was Francis Somers, and added that he was on a visit to a relation of the same name, resident a few miles from X—. He gave us to understand that he was himself studying surgery with the view to a medical appointment in one of the colonies. You are not to suppose, sir, that he had entered thus into his concerns at the first interview; it was not till our acquaintance had ripened, and he had visited our house more than once with my mother's sanction, that these particulars were elicited. He never disguised, from the first, that an attachment to myself was his object originally in introducing himself to our notice. As his prospects were comparatively flattering, my mother did not raise any impediment to his attentions, and I own I received them with pleasure.

' "Days and weeks elapsed; and although the distance at which his relation resided prevented the possibility of an uninterrupted intercourse, yet neither was it so great as to preclude his frequent visits. The interval of a day, or at most of two, was all that intervened, and these temporary absences certainly did not decrease the pleasure of the meetings with which they terminated. At length a pensive expression began to exhibit itself upon his countenance, and I could not but remark that at every visit he became more abstracted and reserved. The eye of affection is not slow to detect any symptom of uneasiness in a quarter dear to it. I spoke to him, questioned him on the subject; his answer was evasive, and I said no more. My mother, too, however, had marked the same appearance of melancholy, and pressed him more strongly. He at length admitted that his spirits were depressed, and that their depression was caused by the necessity of an early, though but a temporary, separation. His uncle, and only friend, he said, had long insisted on his spending some months on the Continent, with the view of completing his professional education, and that the time was now fast approaching when it would be necessary for him to commence his journey. A look made the inquiry which my tongue refused to utter. 'Yes, dearest Mary,' was his reply, 'I have communicated our attachment to him, partially at least; and though I dare not say that the intimation was received as I could have wished, yet I have, perhaps, on the whole, no fair reason to be dissatisfied with his reply.

"'The completion of my studies, and my settlement in the world, must, my uncle told me, be the first consideration; when these material points were achieved, he should not interfere with any arrangement that might be found essential to my happiness: at the same time he has positively refused to sanction any engagement at present, which may, he says, have a tendency to divert my attention from those pursuits, on the due prosecution of which my future situation in life must depend. A compromise between love and duty was eventually wrung from me, though reluctantly; I have pledged myself to proceed immediately to my destination abroad, with a full understanding that on my return, a twelvemonth hence, no obstacle shall be thrown in the way of what are, I trust, our mutual wishes.'

'	"I will not attempt to describe the feelings with which I received this communication, nor will it be necessary to say anything of what passed at the few interviews which took place before Francis quitted X—. The evening immediately previous to that of his departure he passed in this house, and, before we separated, renewed his protestations of an unchangeable affection, requiring a similar assurance from me in return. I did not hesitate to make it. 'Be satisfied, my dear Francis,' said I, 'that no diminution in the regard I have avowed can ever take place, and though absent in body, my heart and soul will still be with you.' – 'Swear this,' he cried, with a suddenness and energy which surprised, and rather startled me: 'promise that you will be with me *in spirit*, at least, when I am far away.' I gave him my hand, but that was not sufficient. 'One of these dark shining ringlets, my dear Mary,' said he, 'as a pledge that you will not forget your vow!' I suffered him to take the scissors from my work-box and to sever a lock of my hair, which he placed in his bosom. – The next day he was pursuing his journey, and the waves were already bearing him from England.

'	"I had letters from him repeatedly during the first three months of his absence; they spoke of his health, his prospects, and of his love, but by degrees the intervals between each arrival became longer, and I fancied I perceived some falling off from that warmth of expression which had at first characterised his communications.

'	"One night I had retired to rest rather later than usual, having sat by the bedside, comparing his last brief note with some of his earlier letters, and was endeavouring to convince myself that my apprehensions of his fickleness were unfounded, when an undefinable sensation of restlessness and anxiety seized upon me. I cannot compare it to anything I had ever experienced before; my pulse fluttered, my heart beat with a quickness and violence which alarmed me, and a strange tremor shook my whole frame. I retired hastily to bed, in hopes of getting rid of so unpleasant a sensation, but in vain; a vague apprehension of I know not what occupied my mind, and vainly did I endeavour to shake it off. I can compare my feelings to nothing but those which we sometimes experience when about to undertake a long and unpleasant journey, leaving those we love behind us. More than once did I raise myself in my bed and listen, fancying that I heard myself called, and on each of those occasions the fluttering of my heart increased. Twice I was on the point of calling to my sister, who then slept in an adjoining room, but she had gone to bed indisposed, and an unwillingness to disturb either her or my mother checked me; the large clock in the room below at this moment began to strike the hour of twelve. I distinctly heard its vibrations, but ere its sounds had ceased, a burning heat, as if a hot iron had been applied to my temple, was succeeded by a dizziness, – a swoon, – a total loss of consciousness as to where or in what situation I was.

' "A pain, violent, sharp, and piercing, as though my whole frame were lacerated by some keen-edged weapon, roused me from this stupor, – but where was I? Everything was strange around me – a shadow dimness rendered every object indistinct and uncertain; methought, however, that I was seated in a large, antique, high-backed chair, several of which were near, their tall black carved frames and seats interwoven with a lattice-work of cane. The apartment in which I sat was one of moderate dimensions, and, from its sloping roof, seemed to be the upper story of the edifice, a fact confirmed by the moon shining without, in full effulgence, on a huge round tower, which its light rendered plainly visible through the open casement, and the summit of which appeared but little superior in elevation to the room I occupied. Rather to the right, and in the distance, the spire of some cathedral or lofty church was visible, while sundry gable-ends, and tops of houses, told me I was in the midst of a populous but unknown city.

' "The apartment itself had something strange in its appearance, and, in the character of its furniture and appurtenances, bore little or no resemblance to any I had ever seen before. The fireplace was large and wide, with a pair of what are sometimes called andirons, betokening the wood was the principal, if not the only fuel consumed within its recess; a fierce fire was now blazing in it, the light from which rendered visible the remotest parts of the chamber. Over a lofty old-fashioned mantelpiece, carved heavily in imitation of fruit and flowers, hung the half-length portrait of a gentleman in a dark-coloured foreign habit, with a peaked beard and moustaches, one hand resting upon a table, the other supporting a sort of *bâton*, or short military staff, the summit of which was surmounted by a silver falcon. Several antique chairs, similar in appearance to those already mentioned, surrounded a massive oaken table, the length of which much exceeded its width. At the lower end of this piece of furniture stood the chair I occupied; on the upper, was placed a small chafing-dish filled with burning coals, and darting forth occasionally long flashes of various-coloured fire, the brilliance of which made itself visible, even above the strong illumination emitted from the chimney. Two huge, black, japanned cabinets, with clawed feet, reflecting from their polished surfaces the effulgence of the flame, were placed one on each side the casement-window to which I have alluded, and with a few shelves loaded with books, many of which were also strewed in disorder on the floor, completed the list of the furniture in the apartment. Some strange-looking instruments, of unknown form and purpose, lay on the table near the chafing-dish, on the other side of which a miniature portrait of myself hung, reflected by a small oval mirror in a dark-coloured frame, while a large open volume, traced with strange characters of the colour of blood, lay in front; a goblet, containing a few drops of liquid of the same ensanguined hue, was by its side.

' "But of the objects which I have endeavoured to describe, none arrested my attention so forcibly as two others. These were the figures of two young men, in the prime of life, only separated from me by the table. They were dressed alike, each in a long flowing gown, made of some sad-coloured stuff, and confined at the waist by a crimson girdle; one of them, the shorter of the two, was occupied in feeding the embers of the chafing-dish with a resinous powder, which produced and maintained a brilliant but flickering blaze, to the action of which his companion was exposing a long lock of dark chestnut hair, that shrank and shrivelled as it approached the flame. But, O God! – that hair! and the form of him who held it! that face! those features! – not for one instant could I entertain a doubt – it was He! Francis! – the lock he grasped was mine, the very pledge of affection I had given him, and still, as it partially encountered the fire, a burning heat seemed to scorch the temple from which it had been taken, conveying a torturing sensation that affected my very brain.

' "How shall I proceed? – but no, it is impossible, – not even to you, sir, can I – dare I – recount the proceedings of that unhallowed night of horror and of shame. Were my life extended to a term commensurate with that of the Patriarchs of old, never could its detestable, its damning pollutions be effaced from my remembrance; and, oh! above all, never could I forget the diabolical glee which sparkled in the eyes of my fiendish tormentors, as they witnessed the worse than useless struggles of their miserable victim. Oh! why was it not permitted me to make refuge in unconsciousness – nay, in death itself, from the abominations of which I was compelled to be, not only a witness, but a partaker? But it is enough, sir; I will not further shock your nature by dwelling longer on a scene, the full horrors of which, words, if I even dared employ any, would be inadequate to express; suffice it to say, that after being subjected to it, how long I knew not, but certainly for more than an hour, a noise from below seemed to alarm my persecutors; a pause ensued, – the lights were extinguished, and, as the sound of a footstep ascending a staircase became more distinct, my forehead felt again the excruciating sensation of heat, while the embers, kindling into a momentary flame, betrayed another portion of the ringlet consuming in the blaze. Fresh agonies succeeded, not less severe, and of a similar description to those which had seized upon me at first: oblivion again followed, and on being at length restored to consciousness, I found myself as you see me now, faint and exhausted, weakened in every limb, and every fibre quivering with agitation. My groans soon brought my sister to my aid; it was long before I could summon resolution to confide, even to her, the dreadful secret, and when I had done so, her strongest efforts were not wanting to persuade me that I had been labouring under a severe attack of nightmare. I ceased to argue, but I was not convinced; the whole scene was then too present, too awfully real, to permit me to doubt the character of the transaction; and if, when a few days had elapsed, the hopelessness of imparting to others the conviction I entertained myself, produced in me an apparent acquiescence with their opinion, I have never been the less satisfied that no cause reducible to the known laws of nature occasioned my sufferings on that hellish evening. Whether that firm belief might have eventually yielded to time, whether I might at length have been brought to consider all that had passed, and the circumstances which I could never cease to remember, as a mere phantasm, the offspring of a heated imagination, acting upon an enfeebled body, I know not – last night, however, would in any case have dispelled the flattering illusion – last night – last night was the whole horrible scene acted over again. The place – the actors – the whole infernal apparatus were the same; the same insults, the same torments, the same brutalities – all were renewed, save that the period of my agony was not so prolonged. I became sensible to an incision in my arm, though the hand that made it was not visible; at the same moment my persecutors paused; they were manifestly disconcerted, and the companion of him, whose name shall never more pass my lips, muttered something to his abettor in evident agitation; the formula of an oath of horrible import was dictated to me in terms fearfully distinct. I refused it unhesitatingly; again and again was it proposed, with menaces I tremble to think on – but I refused; the same sound was heard – interruption was evidently apprehended, – the same ceremony was hastily repeated, and I again found myself released, lying on my own bed, with my mother and my sister weeping over me. O God! O God! when and how is this to end? – When will my spirit be left in peace? – Where, or with whom, shall I find refuge?"

'It is impossible to convey any adequate idea of the emotions with which this unhappy girl's narrative affected me. It must not be supposed that her story was delivered in the same continuous and uninterrupted strain in which I have transcribed its substance. On the contrary, it was not without frequent intervals, of longer or shorter duration, that her account was brought to a conclusion; indeed, many passages of her strange dream were not without the greatest difficulty and reluctance communicated at all. My task was no easy one; never, in the course of a long life spent in the active duties of my Christian calling, – never had I been summoned to such a conference before.

'To the half-avowed, and palliated confession of committed guilt I had often listened, and pointed out the only road to secure its forgiveness. I had succeeded in cheering the spirit of despondency, and sometimes even in calming the ravings of despair; but here I had a different enemy to combat, an ineradicable prejudice to encounter, evidently backed by no common share of superstition, and confirmed by the mental weakness attendant upon severe bodily pain. To argue the sufferer out of an opinion so rooted was a hopeless attempt. I did, however, essay it; I spoke to her of the strong and mysterious connection maintained between our waking images and those which haunt us in our dreams, and more especially during that morbid oppression commonly called nightmare. I was even enabled to adduce myself as a strong and living instance of the excess to which fancy sometimes carries her freaks on those occasions; while, by an odd coincidence, the impression made upon my own mind, which I adduced as an example, bore no slight resemblance to her own. I stated to her, that on my recovery from the fit of epilepsy, which had attacked me about two years since, just before my grandson Frederick, left Oxford, it was with the greatest difficulty I could persuade myself that I had not visited him, during the interval, in his rooms at Brazenose, and even conversed with himself and his friend W—, seated in his arm-chair, and gazing through the window full upon the statue of Cain, as it stands in the centre of the quadrangle.

I told her of the pain I underwent both at the commencement and termination of my attack; of the extreme lassitude that succeeded; but my efforts were all in vain: she listened to me, indeed, with an interest almost breathless, especially when I informed her of my having actually experienced the very burning sensation in the brain alluded to, no doubt a strong attendant symptom of this peculiar affection, and a proof of the identity of the complaint: but I could plainly perceive that I failed entirely in shaking the rooted opinion which possessed her, that her spirit had, by some nefarious and unhallowed means, been actually subtracted for a time from its earthly tenement.'

The next extract which I shall give from my old friend's memoranda is dated August 24th, more than a week subsequent to his first visit at Mrs Graham's. He appears, from his papers, to have visited the poor young woman more than once during the interval, and to have afforded her those spiritual consolations which no one was more capable of communicating. His patient, for so in a religious sense she may well be termed, had been sinking under the agitation she had experienced; and the constant dread she was under of similar sufferings, operated so strongly on a frame already enervated, that life at length seemed to hang only by a thread. His papers go on to say –

'I have just seen poor Mary Graham, – I fear for the last time. Nature is evidently quite worn out; she is aware that she is dying, and looks forward to the termination of her existence here, not only with resignation but with joy. It is clear that her dream, or what she persists in calling her "subtraction", has much to do with this. For the last three days her behaviour has been altered, she has avoided conversing on the subject of her delusion, and seems to wish that I should consider her as a convert to my view of her case. This may, perhaps, be partly owing to the flippancies of her medical attendant upon the subject, for Mr I— has, somehow or other, got an inkling that she has been much agitated by a dream, and thinks to laugh off the impression – in my opinion injudiciously; but though a skilful, and a kind-hearted, he is a young man, and of a disposition, perhaps, rather too mercurial for the chamber of a nervous invalid. Her manner has since been much more reserved to both of us: in my case, probably because she suspects me of betraying her secret.'

'August 26th – Mary Graham is yet alive, but sinking fast; her cordiality towards me has returned since her sister confessed yesterday, that she had herself told Mr I— that his patient's mind "had been affected by a terrible vision". I am evidently restored to her confidence. She asked me this morning, with much earnestness, "What I believed to be the state of departed spirits during the interval between dissolution and the final day of account? And whether I thought they would be safe, in another world, from the influence of wicked persons employing an agency more than human?" Poor child! One cannot mistake the prevailing bias of her mind. Poor child!'

'August 27th – It is nearly over; she is sinking rapidly, but quietly and without pain. I have just administered to her the sacred elements, of which her mother partook. Elizabeth declined doing the same: she cannot, she says, yet bring herself to forgive the villain who has destroyed her sister. It is singular that she, a young woman of good plain sense in ordinary matters, should so easily adopt, and so pertinaciously retain, a superstition so puerile and ridiculous. This must be matter of a future conversation between us; at present, with the form of the dying girl before her eyes, it were vain to argue with her. The mother, I find, has written to young Somers, stating the dangerous situation of his affianced wife; indignant as she justly is, at his long silence, it is fortunate that she has no knowledge of the suspicions entertained by her daughter. I have seen her letter; it is addressed to Mr Francis Somers, in the Hogewoert, at Leyden – a fellow-student, then, of Frederick's. I must remember to inquire if he is acquainted with this young man.'

Mary Graham, it appears, died the same night. Before her departure, she repeated to my friend the singular story she had before told him, without any material variation from the detail she had formerly given. To the last she persisted in believing that her unworthy lover had practised upon her by forbidden arts. She once more described the apartment with great minuteness, and even the person of Francis's alleged companion, who was, she said, about the middle height, hard-featured, with a rather remarkable scar upon his left cheek, extending in a transverse direction from below the eye to the nose. Several pages of my reverend friend's manuscript are filled with reflections upon this extraordinary confession, which, joined with its melancholy termination, seems to have produced no common effect upon him. He alludes to more than one subsequent discussion with the surviving sister, and piques himself on having made some progress in convincing her of the folly of her theory respecting the origin and nature of the illness itself.

His memoranda on this, and other subjects, are continued till about the middle of September, when a break ensues, occasioned, no doubt, by the unwelcome news of his grandson's dangerous state, which induces him to set out forthwith for Holland. His arrival at Leyden was, as I have already said, too late. Frederick S— had expired after thirty hours' intense suffering, from a wound received in a duel with a brother student. The cause of quarrel was variously related; but, according to his landlord's version, it had originated in some silly dispute about a dream of his antagonist's, who had been the challenger. Such, at least, was the account given to him, as he said, by Frederick's friend and fellow lodger, W—, who had acted as second on the occasion, thus acquitting himself of an obligation of the same kind due to the deceased, whose services he had put in requisition about a year before on a similar occasion, when he had himself been severely wounded in the face.

From the same authority I learned that my poor friend was much affected on finding that his arrival had been deferred too long. Every attention was shown him by the proprietor of the house, a respectable tradesman, and a chamber was prepared for his accommodation; the books and few effects of his deceased grandson were delivered over to him, duly inventoried, and, late as it was in the evening when he reached Leyden, he insisted on being conducted immediately to the apartments which Frederick had occupied, there to indulge the first ebullitions of his sorrows, before he retired to his own. Madame Müller accordingly led the way to an upper room, which being situated at the top of the house, had been, from its privacy and distance from the street, selected by Frederick as his study. The Doctor entered, and taking the lamp from his conductress, motioned to be left alone. His implied wish was of course complied with; and nearly two hours had elapsed before his kind-hearted hostess reascended, in the hope of prevailing upon him to return with her, and partake of that refreshment which he had in the first instance peremptorily declined. Her application for admission was unnoticed: – she repeated it more than once, without success; then becoming somewhat alarmed at the continued silence, opened the door and perceived her new inmate stretched on the floor, in a fainting fit. Restoratives were instantly administered, and prompt medical aid succeeded at length in restoring him to consciousness. But his mind had received a shock, from which, during the few weeks he survived, it never entirely recovered. His thoughts wandered perpetually: and though, from the very slight acquaintance which his hosts had with the English language, the greater part of what fell from him remained unknown, yet enough was understood to induce them to believe that something more than the mere death of his grandson had contributed thus to paralyse his faculties.

When his situation was first discovered, a small miniature was found tightly grasped in his right hand. It had been the property of Frederick, and had more than once been seen by the Müllers in his possession. To this the patient made continued reference, and would not suffer it one moment from his sight: it was in his hand when he expired. At my request it was produced to me. The portrait was that of a young woman, in an English morning dress, whose pleasing and regular features, with their mild and somewhat pensive expression, were not, I thought, altogether unknown to me. Her age was apparently about twenty. A profusion of dark chestnut hair was arranged in the Madonna style, above a brow of unsullied whiteness, a single ringlet depending on the left side. A glossy lock of the same colour, and evidently belonging to the original, appeared beneath a small crystal, inlaid in the back of the picture, which was plainly set in gold, and bore in a cipher the letters M. G. with the date 18—. From the inspection of this portrait, I could at the time collect nothing, nor from that of the Doctor himself, which, also, I found the next morning in Frederick's desk, accompanied by two separate portions of hair. One of them was a lock, short, and deeply tinged with grey, and had been taken, I have little doubt, from the head of my old friend himself; the other corresponded in colour and appearance with that at the back of the miniature. It was not till a few days had elapsed, and I had seen the worthy Doctor's remains quietly consigned to the narrow house, that while arranging his papers previous to my intended return upon the morrow, I encountered the narrative I have already transcribed. The name of the unfortunate young woman connected with it forcibly arrested my attention. I recollected it immediately as one belonging to a parishioner of my own, and at once recognised the original of the female portrait as its owner.

I rose not from the perusal of his very singular statement till I had gone through the whole of it. It was late, – and the rays of the single lamp by which I was reading did but very faintly illumine the remoter parts of the room in which I sat. The brilliancy of an unclouded November moon, then some twelve nights old, and shining full into the apartment, did much towards remedying the defect. My thoughts filled with the melancholy details I had read, I rose and walked to the window. The beautiful planet rose high in the firmament, and gave to the snowy roofs of the houses, and pendent icicles, all the sparkling radiance of clustering gems. The stillness of the scene harmonised well with the state of my feelings. I threw open the casement and looked abroad. Far below me, the waters of the principal canal shone like a broad mirror in the moonlight. To the left rose the Burght, a huge round tower of remarkable appearance, pierced with embrasures at its summit; while a little to the right and in the distance, the spire and pinnacles of the Cathedral of Leyden rose in all their majesty, presenting a *coup d'oeil* of surpassing though simple beauty. To a spectator of calm, unoccupied mind, the scene would have been delightful. On me it acted with an electric effect. I turned hastily to survey the apartment in which I had been sitting. It was the one designated as the study of the late Frederick S—. The sides of the room were covered with dark wainscot; the spacious fireplace opposite to me, with its polished andirons, was surmounted by a large old-fashioned mantelpiece, heavily carved in the Dutch style with fruits and flowers; above it frowned a portrait, in a Vandyke dress, with a peaked beard and moustaches; one hand of the figure rested on a table, while the other bore a marshal's staff, surmounted with a silver falcon; and – either my imagination, already heated by the scene, deceived me, – or a smile as of malicious triumph curled the lip and glared in the cold leaden eye that seemed fixed upon my own. The heavy, antique, cane-backed chairs, – the large oaken table, – the bookshelves, the scattered volumes, – all, all were there; while, to complete the picture, to my right and left, as half-breathless I leaned my back against the casement, rose, on each side, a tall, dark ebony cabinet, in whose polished sides the single lamp upon the table shone reflected as in a mirror.

What am I to think? – Can it be that the story I have been reading was written by my poor friend here, and under the influence of delirium? – Impossible! Besides, they all assure me, that from the fatal night of his arrival he never left his bed – never put pen to paper. His very directions to have me summoned from England were verbally given, during one of those few and brief intervals in which reason seemed partially to resume her sway. Can it then be possible that – ? W—?

where is he who alone may be able to throw light on this horrible mystery? No one knows. He absconded, it seems, immediately after the duel. No trace of him exists, nor, after repeated and anxious inquiries, can I find that any student has ever been known in the University of Leyden by the name of Francis Somers.

> '*There are more things in heaven and earth*
> *Than are dreamt of in your philosophy!!*'

The Phantom Regiment

by James Grant

A cousin of Sir Walter Scott, James Grant (1822–1887) was the son of an army captain, a circumstance which was to influence his literary output in no small way. He himself entered the army as an ensign in 1840 but soon resigned his commission to become first a draughtsman and then a writer. His first published work, The Romance of War, or the Highlanders in Spain (1847), *was based on active-service experiences related him by his father. Its success determined him to continue writing about army exploits and he is today best remembered as a military novelist and expert. A prolific writer, in forty years Grant produced twelve historical studies and sixty-one novels. Amongst the latter are* Harry Ogilvie, or the Black Dragoons; The Scottish Cavalier; Jane Seton; The Yellow Frigate; Philip Rollo; Frank Hilton, Legends of the Black Watch; Hollywood House *and* The Adventures of Rob Roy. *Despite this enormous output Grant made little money from his work and died in near-poverty.*

Like his better-known cousin, James Grant was interested in the supernatural and in 1866 produced two notable ghostly tales – The Dead Tryst *and* A Haunted Life. *In* The Phantom Regiment, *which was first published in 1847, Grant combined military knowledge with his taste for the uncanny and produced a powerful darkly-textured story that is not easy to forget.*

THOUGH the continued march of intellect and education have nearly obliterated from the mind of the Scots a belief in the marvellous, still a love of the supernatural lingers among the more mountainous districts of the northern kingdom; for 'the Schoolmaster' finds it no easy task, even when aided by all the light of science, to uproot the prejudices of more than two thousand years.

I was born in Strathnairn, about the year 1802, and, on the death of my mother, was given, when an infant, to the wife of a cotter to nurse. With these good people I remained for some years, and thus became cognizant of the facts I am about to relate.

There was a little romance connected with my old nurse Meinie and her gudeman.

In their younger days they had been lovers—lovers as a boy and girl – but were separated by poverty, and then Ewen Mac Ewen enlisted as a soldier, in the 26th or Cameronian Regiment, with which he saw some sharp service in the West Indies and America. The light-hearted young highlander became, in time, a grave, stern, and morose soldier, with the most rigid ideas of religious deportment and propriety: for this distinguished Scottish regiment was of Puritan origin, being one of those raised among the Westland Covenanters, after the deposition of king James VII by the Estates of Scotland. England surrendered to William of Orange without striking a blow; but the defence of Dunkeld, and the victorious battle of Killycrankie, ended the northern campaign, in which the noble Dundee was slain, and the army of the cavaliers dispersed. The Cameronian Regiment introduced their sectarian forms, their rigorous discipline, and plain mode of public worship into their own ranks, and so strict was their code of morals, that even the Non-jurors and Jacobins admitted the excellence and stern propriety of their bearing. They left the Scottish Service for the British, at the Union, in 1707, but still wear on their appointments the five-pointed star, which was the armorial bearing of the colonel who embodied them; and, moreover, retain the privilege of supplying their own regimental Bibles.

After many years of hard fighting in the old 26th, and after carrying a halbert in the kilted regiment of the Isles, Ewen Mac Ewen returned home to his native place, the great plain of Moray, a graver, and, in bearing, a sadder man than when he left it.

His first inquiry was for Meinie.

She had married a rival of his, twenty years ago.

'God's will be done,' sighed Ewen, as he lifted his bonnet, and looked upwards.

He built himself a little cottage, in the old highland fashion, in his native strath, at a sunny spot, where the Uise Nairn – the Water of Alders – flowed in front, and a wooded hill arose behind. He hung his knapsack above the fireplace; deposited his old and sorely thumbed regimental Bible (with the Cameronian star on its boards,) and the tin case containing his colonel's letter recommending him to the minister, and the discharge, which gave sixpence per diem as the reward of sixteen battles – all on the shelf of the little window, which contained three panes of glass, with a yoke in the centre of each, and there he settled himself down in peace, to plant his own kail, knit his own hose, and to make his own kilts, a grave and thoughtful but contented old fellow, awaiting the time, as he said, 'when the Lord would call him away'.

Now it chanced that a poor widow, with several children, built herself a little thatched house on the opposite side of the drove road – an old Fingalian path – which ascended the pastoral glen; and the ready-handed veteran lent his aid to thatch it, and to sling her kail-pot on the cruicks, and was wont thereafter to drop in of an evening to smoke his pipe, to tell old stories of the storming of Ticonderago, and to ask her little ones the catechism and biblical questions. Within a week or so, he discovered that the widow was Meinie – the ripe, blooming Meinie of other years – an old, a faded, and a sad-eyed woman now; and poor Ewen's lonely heart swelled within him, as he thought of all that had passed since last they met, and as he spake of what they were, and what they might have been, had fate been kind, or fortune proved more true.

55

We have heard much about the hidden and mysterious principle of affinity, and more about the sympathy and sacredness that belong to a first and early love; well, the heart of the tough old Cameronian felt these gentle impulses, and Meinie was no stranger to them. They were married, and for fifteen years, there was no happier couple on the banks of the Nairn. Strange to say, they died on the same day, and were interred in the ancient burying-ground of Dalcross, where now they lie, near the ruined walls of the old vicarage kirk of the Catholic times. God rest them in their humble highland graves! My father, who was the minister of Croy, acted as chief mourner, and gave the customary funeral prayer. But I am somewhat anticipating, and losing the thread of my own story in telling theirs.

In process of time the influx of French and English tourists who came to visit the country of the clans, and to view the plain of Culloden, after the publication of 'Waverley' gave to all Britain, that which we name in Scotland 'the tartan fever', and caused the old path which passed the cot of Ewen to become a turnpike road; a tollbar – that most obnoxious of all impositions to a Celt – was placed across the mouth of the little glen, barring the way directly to the battle-field; and of this gate the old pensioner Ewen naturally became keeper; and during the summer season, when, perhaps, a hundred carriages per day rolled through, it became a source of revenue alike to him, and to the Lord of Cawdor and the Laird of Kilravock, the road trustees. And the chief pleasure of Ewen's existence was to sit on a thatched seat by the gate, for then he felt conscious of being in office – on duty – a species of sentinel; and it smacked of the old time when the Generale was beaten in the morning, and the drums rolled tattoo at night; when he had belts to pipe-clay, and boots to blackball; when there were wigs to frizzle and queues to tie, and to be all trim and in order to meet Monseigneur le Marquis de Montcalm, or General Washington 'right early in the morning'; and there by the new barrier of the glen Ewen sat the live-long day, with spectacles on nose, and the Cameronian Bible on his knee, as he spelled his way through Deuteronomy and the tribes of Judah.

Slates in due time replaced the green thatch of his little cottage; then a diminutive additional story, with two small dormer windows, was added thereto, and the thrifty Meinie placed a paper in her window informing shepherds, the chance wayfarers, and the wandering deer-stalkers that she had a room to let; but summer passed away, the sportsman forsook the brown scorched mountains, the gay tourist ceased to come north, and the advertisement turned from white to yellow, and from yellow to flyblown green in her window; the winter snows descended on the hills, the pines stood in long and solemn ranks by the white frozen Nairn, but 'the room upstairs' still remained without a tenant.

Anon the snow passed away; the river again flowed free, the flowers began to bloom; the young grass to sprout by the hedgerows, and the mavis to sing on the fauld-dykes, for spring was come again, and joyous summer soon would follow; and one night – it was the 26th of April – Ewen was exhibiting his penmanship in large text-hand by preparing the new announcement of 'a room to let', when he paused, and looked up as a peal of thunder rumbled across the sky; a red gleam of lightning flashed in the darkness without, and then they heard the roar of the deep broad Nairn, as its waters, usually so sombre and so slow, swept down from the wilds of Badenoch, flooded with the melting snows of the past winter.

A dreadful storm of thunder, rain, and wind came on, and the little cottage rocked on its foundations; frequently the turf-fire upon the hearth was almost blown about the clay-floor, by the downward gusts that bellowed in the chimney. The lightning gleamed incessantly, and seemed to play about the hill of Urchany and the ruins of Caistel Fionlah; the woods groaned and creaked, and the trees seemed to shriek as their strong limbs were torn asunder by the gusts which in some places laid side by side the green sapling of last summer, and the old oak that had stood for a thousand years – that had seen Macbeth and Duncan ride from Nairn, and had outlived the wars of the Comyns and the Clanehattan.

The swollen Nairn tore down its banks, and swept trees, rocks, and stones in wild confusion to the sea, mingling the pines of Aberarder with the old oaks of Cawdor; while the salt spray from the Moray Firth was swept seven miles inland, where it encrusted with salt the trees, the houses, and windows, and whatever it fell on as it mingled with the ceaseless rain, while deep, hoarse, and loud the incessant thunder rattled across the sky, 'as if all the cannon on earth,' according to Ewen, 'were exchanging salvoes between Urchany and the Hill of Geddes.'

Meinie grew pale, and sat with a finger on her mouth, and a startled expression in her eyes, listening to the uproar without; four children, two of whom were Ewen's, and her last addition to the clan, clung to her skirts.

Ewen had just completed the invariable prayer and chapter for the night, and was solemnly depositing his old regimental companion, with 'Baxter's Saints' Rest,' in a place of security, when a tremendous knock – a knock that rang above the storm – shook the door of the cottage.

'Who can this be, and in such a night?' said Meinie.

'The Lord knoweth,' responded Ewen, gravely; 'but he knocks both loud and late.'

'Inquire before you open,' urged Meinie, seizing her husband's arm, as the impatient knock was renewed with treble violence.

'Who comes there?' demanded Ewen, in a soldierly tone.

'A friend,' replied a strange voice without, and in the same manner.

'What do you want?'

'Fire and smoke!' cried the other, giving the door a tremendous kick; 'do you ask that in such a devil of a night as this? You have a room to let, have you not?'

'Yes.'

'Well; open the door, or blood and 'oons I'll bite your nose off!'

Ewen hastened to undo the door; and then, all wet and dripping as if he had just been fished up from the Moray Firth, there entered a strange-looking old fellow in a red coat; he stumped vigorously on a wooden leg, and carried on his shoulders a box, which he flung down with a crash that shook the dwelling, saying, –

'There – damn you – I have made good my billet at last.'

'So it seems,' said Ewen, reclosing the door in haste to exclude the tempest, lest his house should be unroofed and torn asunder.

'Harkee, comrade, what garrison or fortress is this,' asked the visitor, 'that peaceable folks are to be challenged in this fashion, and forced to give parole and countersign before they march in – eh?'

'It is my house, comrade; and so you had better keep a civil tongue in your head.'

'Civil tongue? Fire and smoke, you mangy cur! I can be as civil as my neighbours; but get me a glass of grog, for I am as wet as we were the night before Minden.'

'Where have you come from in such a storm as this?'

'Where you'd not like to go – so never mind; but, grog, I tell you – get me some grog, and a bit of tobacco; it is long since I tasted either.'

Ewen hastened to get a large quaighful of stiff Glenlivat, which the veteran drained to his health, and that of Meinie; but first he gave them a most diabolical grin, and threw into the liquor some black stuff, saying, –

'I always mix my grog with gunpowder – it's a good tonic; I learned that of a comrade who fell at Minden on the glorious 1st of August, '59.'

'You have been a soldier, then?'

'Right! I was one of the 25th, or old Edinburgh Regiment; they enlisted me, though an Englishman, I believe; for my good old dam was a follower of the camp.'

'Our number was the 26th – the old Cameronian Regiment – so we were near each other, you see, comrade.'

'Nearer than you would quite like, mayhap,' said Wooden-leg, with another grin and a dreadful oath.

'And you have served in Germany?' asked Ewen.

'Germany – aye, and marched over every foot of it, from

59

Hanover to Hell, and back again. I have fought in Flanders, too.'

'I wish you had come a wee while sooner,' said Ewen gravely, for this discourse startled his sense of propriety.

'Sooner,' snarled this shocking old fellow, who must have belonged to that army 'which swore so terribly in Flanders,' as good Uncle Toby says; 'sooner – for what?'

'To have heard me read a chapter, and to have joined us in prayer.'

'Prayers be d—ned!' cried the other, with a shout of laughter, and a face expressive of fiendish mockery, as he gave his wooden leg a thundering blow on the floor; 'fire and smoke – another glass of grog – and then we'll settle about my billet upstairs.'

While getting another dram, which hospitality prevented him from refusing, Ewen scrutinised this strange visitor, whose aspect and attire were very remarkable; but wholly careless of what any one thought, he sat by the hearth, wringing his wet wig, and drying it at the fire.

He was a little man, of a spare, but strong and active figure, which indicated great age; his face resembled that of a rat; behind it hung a long queue that waved about like a pendulum when he moved his head, which was quite bald, and smooth as a cricket-ball, save where a long and livid scar – evidently a sword cut – traversed it. This was visible while he sat drying his wig; but as that process was somewhat protracted, he uttered an oath, and thrust his cocked hat on one side of his head, and very much over his left eye, which was covered by a patch. This head-dress was the old military triple-cocked hat, bound with yellow braid, and having on one side the hideous black leather cockade of the House of Hanover, now happily disused in the British army, and retained as a badge of service by liverymen alone. His attire was an old threadbare red coat, faced with yellow, having square tails and deep cuffs, with braided holes; he wore knee-breeches on his spindle shanks, one of which terminated, as I have said, in a wooden pin; he carried a large knotted stick; and, in outline and aspect, very much resembled, as

Ewen thought, Frederick the Great of Prussia, or an old Chelsea pensioner, or the soldiers he had seen delineated in antique prints of the Flemish wars. His solitary orb possessed a most diabolical leer, and, whichever way you turned, it seemed to regard you with the fixed glare of a basilisk.

'You are a stranger hereabout, I presume?' said Ewen drily.

'A stranger now, certainly; but I was pretty well known in this locality once. There are some bones buried hereabout that may remember me,' he replied, with a grin that showed his fangless jaws.

'Bones!' reiterated Ewen, aghast.

'Yes, bones – Culloden Muir lies close by here, does it not?'

'It does – then you have travelled this road before?'

'Death and the Devil! I should think so, comrade; on this very night sixty years ago I marched along this road, from Nairn to Culloden, with the army of His Royal Highness, the Great Duke of Cumberland, Captain-General of the British troops, in pursuit of the rebels under the Popish Pretender – '

'Under His Royal Highness Prince Charles, you mean, comrade,' said Ewen, in whose breast – Cameronian though he was – a tempest of Highland wrath and loyalty swelled up at these words.

'Prince – ha! ha! ha!' laughed the other; 'had you said as much then, the gallows had been your doom. Many a man I have shot, and many a boy I have brained with the butt end of my musket, for no other crime than wearing the tartan, even as you this night wear it.'

Ewen made a forward stride as if he would have taken the wicked boaster by the throat; his anger was kindled to find himself in presence of a veritable soldier of the infamous 'German Butcher', whose merciless massacre of the wounded clansmen and their defenceless families will never be forgotten in Scotland while oral tradition and written record exist; but Ewen paused, and said in his quiet way, –

'Blessed be the Lord! these times and things have passed away from the land, to return to it no more. We are both old men now; by your own reckoning, you must at least have numbered four-score years, and in that, you are by twenty my better man. You are my guest tonight, moreover, so we must not quarrel, comrade. My father was killed at Culloden.'

'On which side?'

'The right one – for he fell by the side of old Keppoch, and his last words were, "Righ Hamish gu Bragh!"'

'Fire and smoke!' laughed the old fellow, 'I remember these things as if they only happened yesterday – mix me some more grog and put it in the bill – I was the company's butcher in those days – it suited my taste – so when I was not stabbing and slashing the sheep and cattle of the rascally commissary, I was cutting the throats of the Scots and French, for there were plenty of them, and Irish too, who fought against the king's troops in Flanders. We had hot work, that day at Culloden – hotter than at Minden, where we fought in heavy marching order, with our blankets, kettles, and provisions, on a broiling noon, when the battlefield was cracking under a blazing sun, and the whole country was sweltering like the oven of the Great Baker.'

'Who is he?'

'What! you don't know him? Ha! ha! ha! Ho! ho! ho! come, that is good.'

Ewen expostulated with the boisterous old fellow on this style of conversation, which, as you may easily conceive, was very revolting to the prejudices of a well-regulated Cameronian soldier.

'Come, come, you old devilskin,' cried the other, stirring up the fire with his wooden leg, till the sparks flashed and gleamed like his solitary eye; 'you may as well sing psalms to a dead horse, as preach to me. Hark how the thunder roars, like the great guns at Carthagena! More grog – put it in the bill – or, halt, d—me! pay yourself,' and he dashed on the table a handful of silver of the reigns of George II, and the Glencoe assassin, William of Orange.

He obtained more whiskey, and drank it raw, seasoning it from time to time with gunpowder, just as an Arab does his cold water with ginger.

'Where did you lose your eye, comrade?'

'At Culloden; but I found the fellow who pinked me, next day, as he lay bleeding on the field; he was a Cameron, in a green velvet jacket, all covered with silver; so I stripped off his lace, as I had seen my mother do, and then I brained him with the butt-end of brown-bess – and before his wife's eyes, too! What the deuce do you growl at, comrade? Such things will happen in war, and you know that orders must be obeyed. My eye was gone – but it was the left one, and I was saved the trouble of closing it when taking aim. This slash on the sconce I got at the battle of Preston Pans, from the Celt who slew Colonel Gardiner.'

'That Celt was my father – the Miller of Invernahyle,' said Meinie, proudly.

'Your father! fire and smoke! do you say so? His hand was a heavy one!' cried Wooden-leg, while his eye glowed like the orb of a hyaena.

'And your leg?'

'I lost at Minden, in Kingsley's Brigade, comrade; aye, my leg – d—n! – that was indeed a loss.'

'A warning to repentance, I would say.'

'Then you would say wrong. Ugh! I remember when the shot – a twelve-pounder – took me just as we were rushing with charged bayonets on the French cannoniers. Smash! my leg was gone, and I lay sprawling and bleeding in a ploughed field near the Weser, while my comrades swept over me with a wild hurrah! the colours waving, and drums beating a charge.'

'And what did you do?'

'I lay there and swore, believe me.'

'That would not restore your limb again.'

'No; but a few hearty oaths relieve the mind; and the mind relieves the body; you understand me, comrade; so there I lay all night under a storm of rain like this, bleeding and sinking; afraid of the knives of the plundering death-hunters, for my mother had been one, and I remembered well how she looked after the wounded, and cured them of their agony.'

'Was your mother one of those infer—' began Mac Ewen.

'Don't call her hard names now, comrade; she died on the day after the defeat at Val; with the Provost Marshal's cord round her neck – a cordon less ornamental than that of St Louis.'

'And your father?'

'Was one of Howard's Regiment; but which the devil only knows, for it was a point on which the old lady, honest woman, had serious doubts herself.'

'After the loss of your leg, of course you left the service?'

'No, I became the company's butcher; but, fire and smoke, get me another glass of grog; take a share yourself, and don't sit staring at me like a Dutch Souterkin conceived of a winter night over a "pot de feu," as all the world knows King William was. Dam! let us be merry together – ha, ha, ha! ho, ho, ho! and I'll sing you a song of the old whig times.'

> ' "O, brother Sandie, hear ye the news,
>   Lillibulero, bullen a la!
> An army is coming sans breeches and shoes,
>   Lillibulero, bullen a la!
>
> ' "To arms! to arms! brave boys to arms!
>   A true British cause for your courage doth ca';
> Country and city against a kilted banditti,
>   Lillibulero, bullen a la!" '

And while he continued to rant and sing the song (once so obnoxious to the Scottish Cavaliers), he beat time with his wooden leg, and endeavoured to outroar the stormy wind and the hiss of the drenching rain. Even Mac Ewen, though he was an old soldier, felt some uneasiness, and Meinie trembled in her heart, while the children clung to her skirts and hid their little faces, as if this singing, riot, and jollity were impious at such a time, when the awful thunder was ringing its solemn peals across the midnight sky.

Although this strange old man baffled or parried every inquiry of Ewen as to whence he had come, and how and why he wore that antiquated uniform, on his making a lucrative offer to take the upper room of the little toll-house for a year – exactly a year – when Ewen thought of his poor pension of sixpence per diem, of their numerous family, and Meinie now becoming old and requiring many little comforts, all scruples were overcome by the pressure of necessity, and the mysterious old soldier was duly installed in the attic, with his corded chest, scratch-wig, and wooden leg; moreover, he paid the first six months' rent in advance, dashing the money – which was all coin of the first and second Georges, on the table with a bang and an oath, swearing that he disliked being indebted to any man.

The next morning was calm and serene; the green hills lifted their heads into the blue and placid sky. There was no mist on the mountains, nor rain in the valley. The flood in the Nairn had subsided, though its waters were still muddy and perturbed; but save this, and the broken branches that strewed the wayside – with an uprooted tree, or a paling laid flat on the ground, there was no trace of yesterday's hurricane, and Ewen heard Wooden-leg (he had no other name for his new lodger) stumping about overhead,–as the old fellow left his bed betimes, and after trimming his queue and wig, pipeclaying his yellow facings, and beating them well with the brush, in a soldier-like way, he descended to breakfast, but, disdaining porridge and milk, broiled salmon and bannocks of barley-meal, he called for a can of stiff grog, mixed it with powder from his wide waistcoat pocket, and drank it off at a draught. Then he imperiously desired Ewen to take his bonnet and staff, and accompany him so far as Culloden, 'because,' said he, 'I have come a long, long way to see the old place again.'

Wooden-leg seemed to gather – what was quite unnecessary to him – new life, vigour, and energy – as they traversed the road that led to the battlefield, and felt the pure breeze of the spring morning blowing on their old and wrinkled faces.

The atmosphere was charmingly clear and serene. In the distance lay the spires of Inverness, and the shining waters of the Moray Firth, studded with sails, and the ramparts of Fort George were seen jutting out at the termination of a long and green peninsula. In the foreground stood the castle of Dalcross, raising its square outline above a wood, which terminates the eastern side of the landscape. The pine-clad summit of Dun Daviot incloses the west, while on every hand between, stretched the dreary moor of Drummossie – the Plain of Culloden – whilom drenched in the blood of Scotland's bravest hearts.

Amid the purple heath lie two or three grass-covered mounds.

These are the graves of the dead – the graves of the loyal Highlanders, who fell on that disastrous field, and of the wounded, who were so mercilessly murdered next day by an order of Cumberland, which he pencilled on the back of a card (the Nine of Diamonds); thus they were dispatched by platoons, stabbed by bayonets, slashed by swords and spontoons, or brained by the butt-end of musket and carbine; officers and men were to be seen emulating each other in this scene of cowardice and cold-blooded atrocity, which filled every camp and barrack in Continental Europe with scorn at the name of an English soldier.

Ewen was a Highlander, and his heart filled with such thoughts as these, when he stood by the grassy tombs where the fallen brave are buried with the hopes of the house they died for; he took off his bonnet and stood bare-headed, full of sad and silent contemplation; while his garrulous companion viewed the field with his single eye, that glowed like a hot coal, and pirouetted on his wooden pin in a very remarkable manner, as he surveyed on every side the scene of that terrible encounter, where, after enduring a long cannonade of round shot and grape, the Highland swordsmen, chief and gillie, the noble and the nameless, flung themselves with reckless valour on the ranks of those whom they had already routed in two pitched battles.

'It was an awful day,' said Ewen, in a low voice, but with a gleam in his grey Celtic eye; 'yonder my father fell wounded; the bullet went through his shield and pierced him here, just above the belt; he was living next day, when my mother – a poor wailing woman with a babe at her breast – found him; but an officer of Barrel's Regiment ran a sword twice through his body and killed him; for the orders of the German Duke were, "that no quarter should be given". This spring is named MacGillivray's Well, because here they butchered the dying chieftain who led the MacIntoshes – aye bayonetted him, next day at noon, in the arms of his bonnie young wife and his puir auld mother! The inhuman monsters! I have been a soldier,' continued Ewen, 'and I have fought for my country; but had I stood, that day on this Moor of Culloden, I would have shot the German Butcher, the coward who fled from Flanders – I would, by the God who hears me, though that moment had been my last!'

'Ha, ha, ha! Ho, ho, ho!' rejoined his queer companion. 'It seems like yesterday since I was here; I don't see many changes, except that the dead are all buried, whereas we left them to the crows, and a carriage-road has been cut across the field, just where we seized some women, who were looking among the dead for their husbands, and who – '

'Well?'

Wooden-leg whistled, and gave Ewen a diabolical leer with his snaky eye, as he resumed, –

'I see the ridge where the clans formed line – every tribe with its chief in front, and his colours in the centre, when we, hopeless of victory, and thinking only of defeat, approached them; and I can yet see standing the old stone wall which covered their right flank. Fire and smoke! It was against that wall we placed the wounded, when we fired at them by platoons next day. I finished some twenty rebels there myself.'

Ewen's hand almost caught the haft of his skene-dhu, as he said, hoarsely –

'Old man, do not call them rebels in my hearing, and least of all by the graves where they lie; they were good men and true; if they were in error, they have long since answered to God for it, even as we one day must answer; therefore let us treat their memory with respect, as soldiers should ever treat their brothers in arms who fall in war.'

But Wooden-leg laughed with his strange eldritch yell, and then they returned together to the tollhouse in the glen; but Ewen felt strongly dissatisfied with his lodger, whose conversation was so calculated to shock alike his Jacobitical and his religious prejudices. Every day this sentiment grew stronger, and he soon learned to deplore in his inmost heart having ever accepted the rent, and longed for the time when he should be rid of him; but, at the end of the six months, Wooden-leg produced the rent for the remainder of the year, still in old silver of the two first Georges, with a few Spanish dollars, and swore he would set the house on fire, if Ewen made any more apologies about their inability to make him sufficiently comfortable and so forth; for his host and hostess had resorted to every pretence and expedient to rid themselves of him handsomely.

But Wooden-leg was inexorable.

He had bargained for his billet for a year; he had paid for it; and a year he would stay, though the Lord Justice General of Scotland himself should say nay!

Boisterous and authoritative, he awed every one by his terrible gimlet eye and the volleys of oaths with which he overwhelmed them on suffering the smallest contradiction; thus he became the terror of all; and shepherds crossed the hills by the most unfrequented routes rather than pass the toll-bar, where they vowed that his eye bewitched their sheep and cattle. To every whispered and stealthy inquiry as to where his lodger had come from, and how or why he had thrust himself upon this lonely tollhouse, Ewen could only groan and shrug his shoulders, or reply, –

'He came on the night of the hurricane, like a bird of evil omen; but on the twenty-sixth of April we will be rid of him, please Heaven! It is close at hand, and he shall march then, sure as my name is Ewen Mac Ewen!'

He seemed to be troubled in his conscience, too, or to have strange visitors; for often in stormy nights he was heard swearing or threatening, and expostulating; and once or twice, when listening at the foot of the stair, Ewen heard him shouting and conversing from his window with persons on the road, although the bar was shut, locked, and there was no one visible there.

On another windy night, Ewen and his wife were scared by hearing Wooden-leg engaged in a furious altercation with some one overhead.

'Dog, I'll blow out your brains!' yelled a strange voice.

'Fire and smoke! blow out the candle first – ha, ha, ha! ho, ho, ho!' cried Wooden-leg; then there ensued the explosion of a pistol, a dreadful stamping of feet, with the sound of several men swearing and fighting. To all this Ewen and his wife hearkened in fear and perplexity; at last something fell heavily on the floor, and then all became still, and not a sound was heard but the night wind sighing down the glen.

Betimes in the morning Ewen, weary and unslept, left his bed and ascended to the door of this terrible lodger and tapped gently.

'Come in; why the devil this fuss and ceremony, eh, comrade?' cried a hoarse voice, and there was old Wooden-leg, not lying dead on the floor as Ewen expected, or perhaps hoped; but stumping about in his shirt sleeves, pipe-claying his facings, and whistling the 'Point of War'.

On being questioned about the most unearthly 'row' of last night, he only bade Ewen mind his own affairs, or uttered a volley of oaths, some of which were Spanish, and mixing a can of gunpowder grog drained it at a draught.

He was very quarrelsome, dictatorial, and scandalously irreligious; thus his military reminiscences were of so ferocious and blood-thirsty a nature, that they were sufficient to scare any quiet man out of his seven senses. But it was more particularly in relating the butcheries, murders, and ravages of Cumberland in the highlands, that he exulted, and there was always a terrible air of probability in all he said. On Ewen once asking of him if he had ever been punished for the many irregularities and cruelties he so freely acknowledged having committed, –

'Punished? Fire and smoke, comrade, I should think so; I have been flogged till the bones of my back stood through the quivering flesh; I have been picquetted, tied neck and heels, or sent to ride the wooden horse, and to endure other punishments which are now abolished in the king's service. An officer once tied me neck and heels for eight and forty hours – ay, damme, till I lost my senses; but he lost his life soon after, a shot from the rear killed him; you understand me, comrade: ha, ha, ha! ho, ho, ho! a shot from the rear.'

'You murdered him?' said Ewen, in a tone of horror.

'I did not say so,' cried Wooden-leg with an oath, as he dealt his landlord a thwack across the shins with his stump; 'but I'll tell you how it happened. I was on the Carthagena expedition in '41, and served amid all the horrors of that bombardment, which was rendered unsuccessful by the quarrels of the general and admiral; then the yellow fever broke out among the troops, who were crammed on board the ships of war like figs in a cask, or like the cargo of a slaver, so they died in scores – and in scores their putrid corpses lay round the hawsers of the shipping, which raked them up every day as they swung round with the tide; and from all the open gunports, where their hammocks were hung, our sick men saw the ground sharks gorging themselves on the dead, while they daily expected to follow. The air was black with flies, and the scorching sun seemed to have leagued with the infernal Spaniards against us. But, fire and smoke, mix me some more grog, I am forgetting my story!

'Our Grenadiers, with those of other regiments, under Colonel James Grant of Carron, were landed on the Island of Tierrabomba, which lies at the entrance of the harbour of Carthagena, where we stormed two small forts which our ships had cannonaded on the previous day.

' "Grenadiers – open your pouches – handle grenades – blow your fuses!" cried Grant, "forward."

'And then we bayonetted the dons, or with the clubbed musket smashed their heads like ripe pumpkins, while our fleet, anchored with broadsides to the shore, threw shot and shell, grape, cannister, carcasses, and hand-grenades in showers among the batteries, booms, cables, chains, ships of war, gunboats, and the devil only knows what more.

'It was evening when we landed, and as the ramparts of San Luiz de Bocca Chica were within musket shot of our left flank, the lieutenant of our company was left with twelve grenadiers (of whom I was one) as a species of out-picquet to watch the Spaniards there, and to acquaint the officer in the captured forts if anything was essayed by way of sortie.

'About midnight I was posted as an advanced sentinel, and ordered to face La Bocca Chica with all my ears and eyes open. The night was close and sultry; there was not a breath of wind stirring on the land or waveless sea; and all was still save the cries of the wild animals that preyed upon the unburied dead, or the sullen splash caused by some half-shrouded corpse, as it was launched from a gun-port, for our ships were moored within pistol-shot of the place where I stood.

'Towards the west the sky was a deep and lurid red, as if the midnight sea was in flames at the horizon; and between me and this fiery glow, I could see the black and opaque outline of the masts, the yards, and the gigantic hulls of those floating charnel-houses our line-of-battle ships, and the dark solid ramparts of San Luiz de Bocca Chica.

'Suddenly I saw before me the head of a Spanish column!

'I cocked my musket, they seemed to be halted in close order, for I could see the white coats and black hats of a single company only. So I fired at them point blank, and fell back on the picquet, which stood to arms.

'The lieutenant of our grenadiers came hurrying towards me.

'"Where are the dons?" said he.

'"In our front, sir," said I, pointing to the white line which seemed to waver before us in the gloom under the walls of San Luiz, and then it disappeared.

'"They are advancing," said I.

'"They have vanished, fellow," said the lieutenant, angrily.

'"Because they have marched down into a hollow."

'In a moment after they reappeared, upon which the lieutenant brought up the picquet, and after firing three volleys retired towards the principal fort where Colonel

Grant had all the troops under arms; but not a Spaniard approached us, and what, think you, deceived me and caused this alarm? Only a grove of trees, fire and smoke! yes, it was a grove of manchineel trees, which the Spaniards had cut down or burned to within five feet of the ground; and as their bark is white it resembled the Spanish uniform, while the black burned tops easily passed for their grenadier caps to the overstrained eyes of a poor anxious lad, who found himself under the heavy responsibility of an advanced sentinel for the first time in his life.'

'And was this the end of it?' asked Ewen.

'Hell and Tommy?' roared Wooden-leg, 'no – but you shall hear. I was batooned by the lieutenant; then I was tried at the drumhead for causing a false alarm, and sentenced to be tied neck and heels, and lest you may not know the fashion of this punishment I shall tell you of it. I was placed on the ground; my firelock was put under my hams, and another was placed over my neck; then the two were drawn close together by two cartouch-box straps; and in this situation, doubled up as round as a ball, I remained with my chin wedged between my knees until the blood spouted out of my mouth, nose, and ears, and I became insensible. When I recovered my senses the troops were forming in column, preparatory to assaulting Fort San Lazare; and though almost blind, and both weak and trembling, I was forced to take my place in the ranks; and I ground my teeth as I handled my musket and saw the lieutenant of our company, in lace-ruffles and powdered wig, prepare to join the forlorn hope, which was composed of six hundred chosen grenadiers, under Colonel Grant, a brave Scottish officer. I loaded my piece with a charmed bullet, cast in a mould given to me by an Indian warrior, and marched on with my section. The assault failed. Of the forlorn hope I alone escaped, for Grant and his Grenadiers perished to a man in the breach. There, too, lay our lieutenant. A shot had pierced his head behind, just at the queue. Queer, was it not? when I was his covering file?'

As he said this, Wooden-leg gave Ewen another of those

diabolical leers, which always made his blood run cold, and continued, –

'I passed him as he lay dead, with his sword in his hand, his fine ruffled shirt and silk waistcoat drenched with blood – by the bye, there was a pretty girl's miniature, with powdered hair peeping out of it too. "Ho, ho!" thought I, as I gave him a hearty kick; "you will never again have me tied neck-and-heels for not wearing spectacles on sentry, or get me a hundred lashes, for not having my queue dressed straight to the seam of my coat".'

'Horrible!' said Ewen.

'I will wager my wooden leg against your two of flesh and bone, that your officer would have been served in the same way, if he had given you the same provocation.'

'Heaven forbid!' said Ewen.

'Ha, ha, ha! Ho, ho, ho!' cried Wooden-leg.

'You spoke of an Indian warrior,' said Ewen, uneasily, as the atrocious anecdotes of this hideous old man excited his anger and repugnance; 'then you have served, like myself, in the New World?'

'Fire and smoke! I should think so; but long before your day.'

'Then you fought against the Cherokees?'

'Yes.'

'At Warwomans Creek?'

'Yes; I was killed there.'

'You were – what?' stammered Ewen.

'Killed there.'

'Killed?'

'Yes, scalped by the Cherokees; dam! don't I speak plain enough?'

'He is mad,' thought Ewen.

'I am not mad,' said Wooden-leg gruffly.

'I never said so,' urged Ewen.

'Thunder and blazes! but you thought it, which is all the same.'

Ewen was petrified by this remark, and then Wooden-leg, while fixing his hyaena-like eye upon him, and mixing a fresh can of his peculiar grog, continued thus, –

'Yes, I served in the Warwomans Creek expedition in '60. In the preceding year I had been taken prisoner at Fort Ninety-six, and was carried off by the Indians. They took me into the heart of their own country, where an old Sachem protected me, and adopted me in place of a son he had lost in battle. Now this old devil of a Sachem had a daughter – a graceful, pretty and gentle Indian girl, whom her tribe named the Queen of the Beaver dams. She was kind to me, and loved to call me her pale-faced brother. Ha, ha, ha! Ho, ho, ho! Fire and smoke! Do I now look like a man that could once attract a pretty girl's eye, – now, with my wooden-leg, patched face and riddled carcase? Well, she loved me, and I pretended to be in love too, though I did not care for her the value of an old snapper. She was graceful and round in every limb, as a beautiful statue. Her features were almost regular – her eyes black and soft; her hair hung nearly to her knees, while her smooth glossy skin, was no darker than a Spanish brunette's. Her words were like notes of music, for the language of the Cherokees, like that of the Iroquois, is full of the softest vowels. This Indian girl treated me with love and kindness, and I promised to become a Cherokee warrior, a thundering turtle and scalp-hunter for her sake – just as I would have promised anything to any other woman, and had done so a score of times before. I studied her gentle character in all its weak and delicate points, as a general views a fortress he is about to besiege, and I soon knew every avenue to the heart of the place. I made my approaches with modesty, for the mind of the Indian virgin was timid, and as pure as the new fallen snow. I drew my parallels and pushed on the trenches whenever the old Sachem was absent, smoking his pipe and drinking fire-water at the council of the tribe; I soon reached the base of the glacis and stormed the breast-works – dam! I did, comrade.

'I promised her everything, if she would continue to love me, and swore by the Great Spirit to lay at her feet the scalp-lock of the white chief, General the Lord Amherst,

K.C.B., and all that, with every other protestation that occurred to me at the time; and so she soon loved me – and me alone – as we wandered on the green slopes of Tennessee, when the flowering forest-trees, and the magnolias, the crimson strawberries, and the flaming azalea made the scenery beautiful; and where the shrill cry of the hawk, and the carol of the merry mocking-bird, filled the air with sounds of life and happiness.

'We were married in the fantastic fashion of the tribe, and the Indian girl was the happiest squaw in the Beaver dams. I hoed cotton and planted rice; I cut rushes that she might plait mats and baskets; I helped her to weave wampum, and built her a wig-wam, but I longed to be gone, for in six months I was wearied of her and the Cherokees too. In short, one night, I knocked the old Sachem on the head, and without perceiving that he still breathed, pocketed his valuables, such as they were, two necklaces of amber beads and two of Spanish dollars, and without informing my squaw of what I had done, I prevailed upon her to guide me far into the forest, on the skirts of which lay a British outpost, near the lower end of the vale, through which flows the Tennessee River. She was unable to accompany me more than a few miles, for she was weak, weary, and soon to become a mother; so I gave her the slip in the forest, and, leaving her to shift for herself, reached headquarters, just as the celebrated expedition from South Carolina was preparing to march against the Cherokees.

'Knowing well the localities, I offered myself as a guide, and was at once accepted – '

'Cruel and infamous!' exclaimed honest Ewen, whose chivalric Highland spirit fired with indignation at these heartless avowals; 'and the poor girl you deceived – '

'Bah! I thought the wild beasts would soon dispose of her.'

'But then the infamy of being a guide, even for your comrades, against those who had fed and fostered, loved and protected you! By my soul, this atrocity were worthy of King William and his Glencoe assassins!'

'Ho, ho, ho! fire and smoke! you shall hear.

75

'Well, we marched from New York in the early part of 1760. There were our regiment, with four hundred of the Scots Royals, and Montgomery's Highlanders. We landed at Charleston, and marched up the country to Fort Ninety-six on the frontier of the Cherokees. Our route was long and arduous, for the ways were wild and rough, so it was the first of June before we reached Twelve-mile River. I had been so long unaccustomed to carry my knapsack, that its weight rendered me savage and ferocious, and I cursed the service and my own existence; for in addition to our muskets and accoutrements, our sixty rounds of ball cartridge per man, we carried our own tents, poles, pegs, and cooking utensils. Thunder and blazes! when we halted, which we did in a pleasant valley, where the great shady chestnuts and the flowering hickory made our camp alike cool and beautiful, my back and shoulders were nearly skinned; for as you must know well, comrade, the knapsack straps are passed so tightly under the armpits, that they stop the circulation of the blood, and press upon the lungs almost to suffocation. Scores of our men left the ranks on the march, threw themselves down in despair, and were soon tomahawked and scalped by the Indians.

'We marched forward next day, but without perceiving the smallest vestige of an Indian trail; thus we began to surmise that the Cherokees knew not that we were among them; but just as the sun was sinking behind the blue hills, we came upon a cluster of wig-wams, which I knew well; they were the Beaver dams, situated on a river, among wild woods that never before had echoed to the drum or bugle.

'Bad and wicked as I was, some strange emotions rose within me at this moment. I thought of the Sachem's daughter – her beauty – her love for me, and the child that was under her bosom when I abandoned her in the vast forest through which we had just penetrated; but I stifled all regret, and heard with pleasure the order to "examine flints and priming".

'Then the Cherokee warwhoop pierced the echoing sky; a scattered fire was poured upon us from behind the rocks and trees; the sharp steel tomahawks came flashing and whirling through the air; bullets and arrows whistled, and rifles rung, and in a moment we found ourselves surrounded by a living sea of dark-skinned and yelling Cherokees, with plumes on their scalp locks, their fierce visages streaked with war paint, and all their moccasins rattling.

'Fire and fury, such a time it was!

'We all fought like devils, but our men fell fast on every side; the Royals lost two lieutenants, and several soldiers whose scalps were torn from their bleeding skulls in a moment. Our regiment, though steady under fire as a battalion of stone statues, now fell into disorder, and the brown warriors, like fiends in aspect and activity, pressed on with musket and war-club brandished, and with such yells as never rang in mortal ears elsewhere. The day was lost, until the Highlanders came up, and then the savages were routed in an instant, and cut to pieces. "Shoot and slash" was the order; and there ensued such a scene of carnage as I had not witnessed since Culloden, where His Royal Highness, the fat Duke of Cumberland, galloped about the field, overseeing the wholesale butchery of the wounded.

'We destroyed their magazines of powder and provisions; we laid the wig-wams in ashes, and shot or bayonetted every living thing, from the babe on its mother's breast, to the hen that sat on the roost; for as I had made our commander aware of all the avenues, there was no escape for the poor devils of Cherokees. Had the pious, glorious, and immortal King William been there, he would have thought we had modelled the whole affair after his own exploit at Glencoe.

'All was nearly over, and among the ashes of the smoking wigwams and the gashed corpses of king's soldiers and Indian warriors, I sat down beneath a great chestnut to wipe my musket, for butt, barrel, and bayonet were clotted with blood and human hair – ouf, man, why do you shudder? it was only Cherokee wool; – all was nearly over, I have said, when a low fierce cry, like the hoarse hiss of a serpent, rang in my ear; a brown and bony hand clutched my throat as the fangs of a wolf would have done, and hurled me to the earth!

A tomahawk flashed above me, and an aged Indian's face, whose expression, was like that of a fiend, came close to mine, and I felt his breath upon my cheek. It was the visage of the sachem, but hollow with suffering and almost green with fury, and he laughed like a hyaena, as he poised the uplifted axe.

'Another form intervened for a moment; it was that of the poor Indian girl I had so heartlessly deceived; she sought to stay the avenging hand of the frantic sachem; but he thrust her furiously aside, and in the next moment the glittering tomahawk was quivering in my brain – a knife swept round my head – my scalp was torn off, and I remember no more.'

'A fortunate thing for you,' said Ewen, drily; 'memory such as yours were worse than a knapsack to carry; and so you were killed there?'

'Don't sneer, comrade,' said Wooden-leg, with a diabolical gleam in his eye; 'prithee, don't sneer; I was killed there, and, moreover, buried too, by the Scots Royals, when they interred the dead next day.'

'Then how came you to be here?' said Ewen, not very much at ease, to find himself in company with one he deemed a lunatic.

'Here? that is my business – not yours,' was the surly rejoinder.

Ewen was silent, but reckoned over that now there were but thirty days to run until the 26th of April, when the stipulated year would expire.

'Yes, comrade, just thirty days,' said Wooden-leg, with an affirmative nod, divining the thoughts of Ewen; 'and then I shall be off, bag and baggage, if my friends come.'

'If not?'

'Then I shall remain where I am.'

'The Lord forbid!' thought Ewen; 'but I can apply to the sheriff.'

'Death and fury! Thunder and blazes! I should like to see the rascal of a sheriff who would dare to meddle with me!' growled the old fellow, as his one eye shot fire, and, limping away, he ascended the stairs grumbling and swearing, leaving poor Ewen terrified even to think, on finding that his thoughts, although only half conceived, were at once divined and responded to by this strange inmate of his house.

'His friends,' thought Ewen, 'who may they be?'

Three heavy knocks rang on the floor overhead, as a reply. It was the wooden leg of the Cherokee invader.

This queer old fellow (continued the quarter-master) was always in a state of great excitement, and used an extra number of oaths, and mixed his grog more thickly with gunpowder, when a stray red coat appeared far down the long green glen, which was crossed by Ewen's lonely toll-bar. Then he would get into a prodigious fuss and bustle, and was wont to pack and cord his trunk, to brush up his well-worn and antique regimentals, and to adjust his queue and the black cockade of his triple-cornered hat, as if preparing to depart.

As the time of that person's wished-for departure drew nigh, Ewen took courage, and shaking off the timidity with which the swearing and boisterous fury of Wooden-leg had impressed him, he ventured to expostulate a little on the folly and sin of his unmeaning oaths, and the atrocity of the crimes he boasted of having committed.

But the wicked old Wooden-leg laughed and swore more than ever, saying that a 'true soldier was never a religious one.'

'You are wrong, comrade,' retorted the old Cameronian, taking fire at such an assertion; 'religion is the lightest burden a poor soldier can carry; and, moreover, it hath upheld me on many a long day's march, when almost sinking under hunger and fatigue, with my pack, kettle, and sixty rounds of ball ammunition on my back. The duties of a good and brave soldier are no way incompatible with those of a Christian man; and I never lay down to rest on the wet bivouac or bloody field, with my knapsack, or it might be a dead comrade, for a pillow, without thanking God –'

'Ha, ha, ha!'

' – The God of Scotland's covenanted Kirk for the mercies

79

he vouchsafed to Ewen Mac Ewen, a poor grenadier of the 26th Regiment.'

'Ho, ho, ho!'

The old Cameronian took off his bonnet and lifted up his eyes, as he spoke fervently, and with the simple reverence of the olden time; but Wooden-leg grinned and chuckled and gnashed his teeth as Ewen resumed.

'A brave soldier may rush to the cannon's mouth, though it be loaded with grape and cannister; or at a line of levelled bayonets – and rush fearlessly too – and yet he may tremble without shame, at the thought of hell, or of offended Heaven. Is it not so, comrade? I shall never forget the words of our chaplain before we stormed the Isles of Saba and St Martin from the Dutch, with Admiral Rodney, in '81.'

'Bah – that was after I was killed by the Cherokees. Well?'

'The Cameronians were formed in line, mid leg in the salt water, with bayonets fixed, the colours flying, the pipes playing and drums beating "Britons strike home", and our chaplain, a reverend minister of God's word, stood beside the colonel with the shot and shell from the Dutch batteries flying about his old white head, but he was cool and calm, for he was the grandson of Richard Cameron, the glorious martyr of Airdsmoss.

' "Fear not, my bairns," cried he (he aye called us his bairns, having ministered unto us for fifty years and more) – "fear not; but remember that the eyes of the Lord are on every righteous soldier, and that His hand will shield him in the day of battle!"

' "Forward, my lads," cried the colonel, waving his broad sword, while the musket shot shaved the curls of his old brigadier wig; "forward, and at them with your bayonets"; and bravely we fell on – eight hundred Scotsmen, shoulder to shoulder – and in half an hour the British flag was waving over the Dutchman's Jack on the ramparts of St Martin.'

But to all Ewen's exordiums, the Wooden-leg replied by oaths, or mockery, or his incessant laugh, –

'Ha, ha, ha! Ho, ho, ho!'

At last came the long-wished for twenty-sixth of April!

The day was dark and louring. The pine woods looked black, and the slopes of the distant hills seemed close and near, and yet gloomy withal. The sky was veiled by masses of hurrying clouds, which seemed to chase each other across the Moray Firth. That estuary was flecked with foam, and the ships were riding close under the lee of the Highland shore, with topmasts struck, their boats secured, and both anchors out, for everything betokened a coming storm.

And with night it came in all its fury; – a storm similar to that of the preceding year.

The fierce and howling wind swept through the mountain gorges, and levelled the lonely shielings, whirling their fragile roofs into the air, and uprooting strong pines and sturdy beeches; the water was swept up from the Loch of the Clans, and mingled with the rain which drenched the woods around it. The green and yellow lightning played in ghastly gleams about the black summit of Dun Daviot, and again the rolling thunder bellowed over the graves of the dead on the bleak, dark moor of Culloden. Attracted by the light in the windows of the toll house, the red deer came down from the hills in herds and cowered near the little dwelling; while the cries of the affrighted partridges, blackcocks, and even those of the gannets from the Moray Firth were heard at times, as they were swept past, with branches, leaves, and stones, on the skirts of the hurrying blast.

'It is just such a storm as we had this night twelvemonths ago,' said Meinie, whose cheek grew pale at the elemental uproar.

'There will be no one coming up the glen tonight,' replied Ewen; 'so I may as well secure the toll-bar, lest a gust should dash it to pieces.'

It required no little skill or strength to achieve this in such a tempest; the gate was strong and heavy, but it was fastened at last, and Ewen retreated to his own fireside. Meanwhile, during all this frightful storm without, Wooden-leg was heard singing and carolling upstairs, stumping about in the lulls of the tempest, and rolling, pushing, and tumbling his chest from side to side; then he descended to get a fresh can of grog – for 'grog, grog, grog,' was ever his cry. His old withered face was flushed, and his excited eye shone like a baleful star. He was conscious that a great event would ensue.

Ewen felt happy in his soul that his humble home should no longer be the resting-place of this evil bird whom the last tempest had blown hither.

'So you leave us tomorrow, comrade?' said he.

'I'll march before daybreak,' growled the other; ''twas our old fashion in the days of Minden. Huske and Hawley always marched off in the dark.'

'Before daybreak?'

'Fire and smoke, I have said so, and you shall see; for my friends are on the march already; but good night, for I shall have to parade betimes. They come; though far, far off as yet.'

He retired with one of his diabolical leers, and Ewen and his wife ensconced themselves in the recesses of their warm box-bed; Meinie soon fell into a sound sleep, though the wind continued to howl, the rain to lash against the trembling walls of the little mansion, and the thunder to hurl peal after peal across the sky of that dark and tempestuous night.

The din of the elements and his own thoughts kept Ewen long awake; but though the gleams of electric light came frequent as ever through the little window, the glow of the 'gathering peat' sank lower on the hearth of hard-beaten clay, and the dull measured tick-tack of the drowsy clock as it fell on the drum of his ear, about midnight, was sending him to sleep, by the weariness of its intense monotony, when from a dream that the fierce hawk eye of his malevolent lodger was fixed upon him, he started suddenly to full consciousness. An uproar of tongue now rose and fell upon the gusts of wind without; and he heard an authoritative voice requiring the toll-bar to be opened.

Overhead rang the stumping of the Wooden-leg, whose hoarse voice was heard bellowing in reply from the upper window.

'The Lord have a care of us!' muttered Mac Ewen, as he threw his kilt and plaid round him, thrust on his bonnet and brogues, and hastened to the door, which was almost blown in by the tempest as he opened it.

The night was as dark, and the hurricane as furious as ever; but how great was Ewen's surprise to see the advanced guard of a corps of Grenadiers, halted at the toll-bar gate, which he hastened to unlock, and the moment he did so, it was torn off its iron hooks and swept up the glen like a leaf from a book, or a lady's handkerchief; as with an unearthly howling the wind came tearing along in fitful and tremendous gusts, which made the strongest forests stoop, and dashed the struggling coasters on the rocks of the Firth – the Æstuarium Vararis of the olden time.

As the levin brands burst in lurid fury overhead, they seemed to strike fire from the drenched rocks, the dripping trees, and the long line of flooded roadway, that wound through the pastoral glen towards Culloden.

The advanced guard marched on in silence with arms slung; and Ewen, to prevent himself from being swept away by the wind, clung with both hands to a stone pillar of the bar gate, that he might behold the passage of this midnight regiment, which approached in firm and silent order in sections of twelve files abreast, all with muskets slung. The pioneers were in front, with their leather aprons, axes, saws, bill-hooks, and hammers; the band was at the head of the column; the drums, fifes, and colours were in the centre; the captains were at the head of their companies; the subalterns on the reverse flank, and the field-officers were all mounted on black chargers, that curvetted and pranced like shadows, without a sound.

Slowly they marched, but erect and upright, not a man of them seeming to stoop against the wind or rain, while overhead the flashes of the broad and blinding lightning were blazing like a ghastly torch, and making every musket-barrel, every belt-plate, sword-blade, and buckle, gleam as this mysterious corps filed through the barrier, with who? Wooden-leg among them!

By the incessant gleams Ewen could perceive that they were Grenadiers, and wore the quaint old uniform of George II's time; the sugar-loaf-shaped cap of red cloth embroidered with worsted; the great square-tailed red coat with its heavy cuffs and close-cut collar; the stockings rolled above the knee, and enormous shoe-buckles. They carried grenado-pouches; the officers had espontoons; the sergeants shouldered heavy halberds, and the coats of the little drum-boys were covered with fantastic lace.

It was not the quaint and antique aspect of this solemn battalion that terrified Ewen, or chilled his heart; but the ghastly expression of their faces, which were pale and hollow-eyed, being, to all appearance, the visages of spectres; and they marched past like a long and wavering panorama, without a sound; for though the wind was loud, and the rain was drenching, neither could have concealed the measured tread of so many mortal feet; but there was no footfall heard on the roadway, nor the tramp of a charger's hoof; the regiment defiled past, noiseless as a wreath of smoke.

The pallor of their faces, and the stillness which accompanied their march, were out of the course of nature; and the soul of Mac Ewen died away within him; but his eyes were riveted upon the marching phantoms – if phantoms, indeed, they were – as if by fascination; and, like one in a terrible dream, he continued to gaze until the last files were past; and with them rode a fat and full-faced officer, wearing a three-cocked hat, and having a star and blue ribbon on his breast. His face was ghastly like the rest, and dreadfully distorted, as if by mental agony and remorse. Two aides-de-camps accompanied him, and he rode a wild-looking black horse, whose eyes shot fire. At the neck of the fat spectre – for a spectre he really seemed – hung a card.

It was the Nine of Diamonds!

The whole of this silent and mysterious battalion passed in line of march up the glen, with the gleams of lightning flashing about them. One bolt more brilliant than the rest brought back the sudden flash of steel.

They had fixed bayonets, and shouldered arms!

84

And on, and on they marched, diminishing in the darkness and the distance, those ghastly Grenadiers, towards the flat bleak moor of Culloden, with the green lightning playing about them, and gleaming on the storm-swept waste.

The Wooden-leg – Ewen's unco' guest – disappeared with them, and was never heard of more in Strathnairn.

He had come with a tempest, and gone with one. Neither was any trace ever seen or heard of those strange and silent soldiers. No regiment had left Nairn that night, and no regiment reached Inverness in the morning; so unto this day the whole affair remains a mystery, and a subject for ridicule with some, although Ewen, whose story of the midnight march of a corps in time of war – caused his examination by the authorities in the Castle of Inverness – stuck manfully to his assertions, which were further corroborated by the evidence of his wife and children. He made a solemn affidavit of the circumstances I have related before the sheriff, whose court books will be found to confirm them in every particular; if not, it is the aforesaid sheriff's fault, and not mine.

There were not a few (but these were generally old Jacobite ladies of decayed Highland families, who form the gossiping tabbies and wall-flowers of the Northern Meeting) who asserted that in their young days they had heard of such a regiment marching by night, once a year to the field of Culloden; for it is currently believed by the most learned on such subjects in the vicinity of the 'Clach na Cudden', that on the anniversary of the sorrowful battle, a *certain place*, which shall be nameless, opens, and that the restless souls of the murderers of the wounded clansmen march in military array to the green graves upon the purple heath, in yearly penance; and this story was thought to receive full corroboration by the apparition of a fat lubberly spectre with the nine of diamonds chained to his neck; as it was on that card – since named the Curse of Scotland – the Duke of Cumberland hastily pencilled the savage order to 'show no quarter to the wounded, but to slaughter all'.

A Night in an Old Castle

by G. P. R. James

George Payne Rainsford James, (1799–1860) whom S. M. Ellis called 'one of the most mysterious figures in Victorian literature', was born in London, the son of a well-to-do physician. Whilst still young, James travelled extensively throughout Europe and was captured by the French at the time of the Napoleonic Wars. During this period he fought a duel with a French officer whom he mortally wounded – an occurrence that was said to haunt him in later life.

James had hoped for a career as a Tory politician but political success evaded him and he turned to writing as a means of support, contributing anonymous articles and stories to magazines. The success of these contributions prompted Washington Irving to encourage him to undertake a more substantial work. The result was Richelieu (1829), *a historical novel which immediately earned James the praise of no less a writer than Sir Walter Scott. From this time, for a period of eighteen years, James produced novels at the rate of one every nine months in addition to a steady flow of poetry, biography and historical writing. In recognition of his historical researches, William IV appointed him Historiographer Royal.*

In all, James wrote fifty six novels, amongst them Darnley (1830), The Gypsey (1835), Attila (1837), The Brigand, or Corse de Leon (1841) *and* The Smuggler (1845.) *In 1847 James produced a novel with the magnificent title of* The Castle of Ehrenstein, Its Lords Spiritual and Temporal, Its Inhabitants Earthly and Unearthly. *As may be imagined, it was a gothic romance firmly in the tradition of Horace Walpole. And so is* A Night in an Old Castle.

It was one of the most awful nights I ever remember having seen. We had set out from St Coar in a carriage which we hired at Cologne, drawn by two black horses, which proved as stubborn and strange a pair of brutes as man could undertake to drive.

Not that I undertook it, for I wanted to see the Rhine from the land route, and not to weary my arms and occupy my attention with an unprofitable pair of dirty reins; but my friend, Mr Lawrence, was rather fond of pulling at horses' mouths and he preferred driving himself, and me too, to being troubled – bored he called it – with a coachman. The landlord of the 'Adler' knew me well, and had no fear of trusting his horses with me, though, to say sooth, I had some fear of trusting myself with them.

I got in, however, beside my friend, and away we went. As far as Bonn all was well enough; but there the horses insisted upon stopping to eat. Lawrence tried to persuade them it would be better to go on; but it was of no use: they had been accustomed to stop at the Star, and stop they would. We made the best of it, fed the horses, and got some dinner ourselves, and then we set out again.

Thus we were at length going along the high and proper road, at a speed dangerous to market men and women, and to our own necks; but even that at length was quieted down, and our further journey only suffered interruption from an occasional dart which both the horses would make at any diverging road that led away from the river, as if they had a presentiment that their course up the stream would lead to something strange and horrible.

About three o'clock we saw a large heavy cloud begin to rise before us, overtopping the mountains, overshadowing the Rhine. It was only in hue that it bore the look of a thundercloud. It had no knobs, or pillars, or writhing twists about it;

but it was inky black, and kept advancing like a wall of marble, dark as night at the lower part, and leaden-grey at the superior edge.

A light wind at length fluttered in our faces, hot and unrefreshing, like the breath of fever.

'Put up the hood!' said Lawrence, 'we are going to have it!'

Hardly had he spoken when a bright flash burst from the cloud, and I could see a serpent-like line of fire dart across the Rhine. Then came a clap of thunder which I thought would bring the rocks and mountains on our heads.

There were two or three more such flashes, and two or three other roars, and then the giant began to weep. Down came the rain like fury: it seemed as if we had got into the middle of a water-spout; and the sky, too, grew so dark that an unnatural shadow filled the whole valley of the Rhine, late so bright and smiling.

At length, to complete our discomforts, night fell; and one so black and murky I have never seen. It was in vain whipping; neither horse would go the least out of his determined pace; and, besides, the whip had become so soaked and limp that it was of little service, moving as unwillingly as the brutes themselves, and curling itself up into a thousand knots.

I got as far back in the carriage as I could, and said nothing. As for my companion he seemed at his wits' end, and I could hear muttered curses which might have well been spared, but which I was in no mood to reprove.

At length he said, 'This will never do! I cannot see a step before me. We shall meet with some accident. Let us get into the first place of shelter we can find. Any cottage, any roadside public-house or beer-house, is better than this.'

'I do not think you will find anything of the kind,' I answered gloomily; 'if you do, I can be contented with any place to get out of this pelting – a cave in the rock if nothing better.'

He drove on nearly at a walk for about two miles further, and then suddenly pulled up. I could hardly see anything but a great black point of rock sticking out, as it seemed to me, right across the road. But Lawrence declared that he perceived a shed under the rock, and a building on the top of it, and asked me to get out and reconnoitre.

I was as glad to catch at straws as he could be, and I alighted as well as I could, stumbling upon a large stone over which he had nearly driven us, and sinking deep in mud and mire. I now found that the rock which had seemed to block the way was only one of those many little points round which the river turns in its course through the mountains, and on approaching near it I discovered the shed he had seen. It was an old dilapidated timber-built hut, which might have belonged at some former period to a boatman, or perhaps a vine-dresser, but it was open at two sides, and we might as well have been in the carriage as there.

By the side, however, I found a path with a step or two cut in the rock, and I judged rightly that it must lead to the building Lawrence had seen above. On returning to the side of the carriage, I clearly perceived the building too, and made it out to be one of the old castles of which such multitudes stud the banks of the frontier river. Some of these, as we all know, are in a very ruinous, some in a more perfect, state; and I proposed to my companion to draw the horses and carriage under the shed, climb the path, and take our chance of what we should find above.

Phaethon himself could not have been more sick of charioteering than Lawrence was: he jumped at the proposal. We secured our vehicle and its brutes as well as we could, and I began to climb. Lawrence stayed a minute behind to get the portmanteau out from under the seat where we had stowed it to keep it dry; and then came hallooing after me with it upon his shoulder.

'Do you think there is a chance of finding anyone up there?' he asked, as he overtook me.

'A chance, certainly; but a poor one,' I answered. 'Marxburg and one or two other old castles are inhabited; but not many. However, we shall soon know; for this one is low down, thank Heaven! and here we are at some gate or barbican.'

I cannot say that it was very promising to the feel – for

sight aided us but little – and the multitude of stones we tumbled over gave no idea of the castle itself being in a high state of repair. Lawrence thought fit to give a loud halloo; but the whistling wind drowned it – and would have drowned it if he had shouted like Achilles from the trenches.

We next had to pick our way across what had probably been a court of the castle; that was an easy matter, for the stones in the open space were few, and the inequalities not many. The moon, I suppose, had risen by this time, for there seemed more light, though the rain ceased not; but we could now perceive several towers and walls quite plainly; and at length I found myself under a deep archway, on one side of which the drifting deluge did not reach me.

As soon as I got under shelter, I extracted my large box of matches and lighted one easily enough. It burned while one might count twenty, but that sufficed to show us that we were under a great gateway between two high towers. A second which I lighted Lawrence carried out into an inner court, but it was extinguished in a moment.

I had perceived, however, a doorway on either side of this arch, and the spikes of a portcullis protruding through the arch above, which showed that the castle had some wood-work left about it; and as soon as he came back we lighted another match, and set out to explore what was behind the two doorways, which we managed easily by getting a new light as soon as the old one was burned out.

On the right there was nothing but one small room, with no exit but the entrance, and with a roof broken in and rank weeds rising from the encumbered floor. On the left was a room of the same size, equally dilapidated, but with a second door and two steps leading to a larger room or hall, the roof of which was perfect except at one end. There were two old lozenge-shaped windows likewise, minus a few panes; but the sills were raised nearly a man's height from the floor, and thus, when one was seated on the ground, one's head was out of the draught.

Comparison is a wonderful thing, and the place looked quite comfortable. Lawrence threw down the portmanteau, and while he held a lighted match, I undid it and got out a wax candle. We had now the means of light till morning, and it remained to get some dry clothing, if it could be found. We had each a dress-suit and a couple of shirts in the portmanteau; and though the rain in one spot had contrived to penetrate the solid leather and wet the shoulder of my coat and the knee of his pantaloons, it was certainly better to have but one damp place of a few inches about one than to be wet all over.

We therefore dressed ourselves in what the apprentice boys would call our best clothes, and a little brandy from the flask made us feel still more comfortable. The taste for luxuries increases with marvellous rapidity under indulgence. An hour before, we should have thought a dry coat and a place of shelter formed the height of human felicity, but now we began to long for a fire on the broad stone hearth at the end of the room.

Lawrence was fertile in resources and keen-sighted enough. He had remarked a quantity of fallen rafters in the first little room we had entered, and he now made sundry pilgrimages thither in the dark – for we dared not take out the candle – till l e had accumulated enough wood to keep us dry all night. Some of it was wet and would not burn, but other pieces were quite dry, and we soon had a roaring fire, by which we sat down on the ground, hoping to make ourselves comfortable.

Oh the vanity of human expectations! As long as we had been busy in repairing our previous disasters we had been well enough; but as soon as we were still – no, not quite so soon as that, but by the time we had stared into the fire for ten minutes, and made out half a dozen pictures on the firebrands, miseries began to press upon us.

'I wish to heaven I had something to sit upon!' said Lawrence, 'if it were but a three-legged stool. My knees get quite cramped.'

'How the wind howls and mourns,' said I, listening. 'It would not surprise me if one half of this old crazy place were to come down upon our heads.'

'The rain is pouring on as heavily as ever,' said Lawrence. 'I should not wonder if that puddle at the other end were to swell into a lake and wash us out at the door.'

'Those poor brutes of horses,' said I, 'must have a bad time of it, and the chaise will be like a full sponge.'

'Come, come!' said Lawrence, 'this will never do. We shall croak ourselves into a fit of the horrors. Let us forget the storm, and the horses, and the old tumbledown place, and fancy ourselves in a middling sort of inn, with a good fire, but little to eat. It is the best policy to laugh at petty evils. Come, can not you tell us a story beginning "Once upon a time"?'

I was in no fit mood for story-telling, but there was some philosophy in his plan, and I accordingly agreed, upon the condition that when I had concluded my narrative he would tell another story.

'Once upon a time,' I said, 'when the late Duke of Hamilton was a young man, and travelling in Italy – making the grand tour, as it was called in those days – he came one night to a solitary inn in the mountains, where he was forced to take refuge from a storm something like that which we have met with today – '

'Oh, I know that story,' cried Lawrence, interrupting me; 'I have heard it a hundred times; and besides, you do not tell it right – My God, what is that?'

As he spoke, he sprang up on his feet with a look of consternation and a face turning suddenly pale.

'What? what?' I cried, 'I heard nothing.'

'Listen!' he said, 'it was certainly a shriek.'

We were silent as death for the next minute, and then again, rising above the moaning wind and pattering rain, came one of the most piercing, agonising shrieks I ever heard. It seemed quite close to where we sat – driven in, as it were, through the broken panes of the casement.

'There must have been some accident,' I said, anxiously. 'Let us go down and see.'

We had contrived to fix our candle between two pieces of firewood, and, leaving it burning, we hurried out through the little ante-room to the old dark archway. The night seemed blacker than ever, and the storm no less severe.

'Stay, stay!' said Lawrence; 'let us listen. We hear nothing to direct us where to search.'

I stopped, and we bent our ears in vain for another sound. We heard the wind sigh, and the rustling patter of the rain, and the roaring of the mighty river as, swollen tremendously, it went roaring along through its rocky channel, but nothing like a human voice made itself heard.

No answer was returned, and again and again he called without obtaining a reply. It was evident that the lips which had uttered those sounds of pain or terror were either far away or still in death; and having nothing to guide us further, we returned to our place of shelter.

At length, quite tired out, I proposed that we should try to sleep. Lawrence ensconced himself behind the door; I took up a position in the other corner, sitting on the floor with my back supported by the two walls, and at a sufficient distance from the window.

I should have said we had piled more wood on the fire, in such a way as we hoped would keep it in at least till we woke; and it flickered and flared and cast strange lights upon the walls and old windows, and upon a door at the other end of the room which we had never particularly examined, on account of the wet and decayed state of the floor in that part.

It was a very common door – a great mass of planks placed perpendicularly and bound together by two great horizontal bars – but as the firelight played upon it, there was something unpleasant to me in its aspect. I kept my eyes fixed upon it, and wondered what was beyond; and, in the sort of unpleasant fancifulness which besets one sometimes when dreary, I began to imagine all sorts of things. It seemed to me to move as if about to be opened; but it was only the shaking of the wind.

It looked like a prison door, I thought – the entrance to some unhappy wretch's cell; and when I was half asleep, I asked myself if there could be anyone there still – could the shrieks we heard issue thence – or could the spirit of the tortured captive still come back to mourn over the sorrows endured in life? I shut my eyes to get rid of the sight of it; but when I opened them again, there it was staring me full in the face.

Sometimes when the flame subsided indeed, I lost sight of it; but that was as bad or worse than the full view, for then I could not tell whether it was open or shut. But at length, calling myself a fool, I turned away from it, and soon after dozed off to sleep.

I could not have been really in slumber more than an hour, and was dreaming that I had just been carried off a road into a river, and just heard all the roaring and rushing of a torrent in my ears, when Lawrence woke me by shaking me violently by the shoulder, and exclaiming: 'Listen, listen! What in the fiend's name can all that be?'

I started up bewildered; but in a moment I heard sounds such as I never heard before in my life; frantic yells and cries, and groans even – all very different from the shrieks we had heard before. Then, suddenly, there was a wild peal of laughter ringing all through the room, more terrible than the rest.

I cannot bear to be wakened suddenly out of sleep; but to be roused by such sounds as that quite overcame me, and I shook like a leaf. Still, my eyes turned towards the door at the other end of the room. The fire had sunk low; the rays of our solitary candle did not reach it, but there was now another light upon it, fitful as the flickering of the flame, but paler and colder. It seemed blue almost to me. But as soon as I could recall my senses I perceived that the moon was breaking the clouds, and from time to time shining through the casement as the scattered vapours were hurried over her by the wind.

'What in Heaven's name can it be?' I exclaimed, quite aghast.

'I don't know, but we must see,' answered my companion, who had been awake longer and recovered his presence of mind. 'Light the other candle, and bring the one that is alight. We must find out what this is. Some poor creature may be wanting help.'

'The sound comes from beyond that door;' I said: 'let us see what is behind it.'

I acknowledge I had some trepidation in making the proposal, but my peculiar temperament urged me forward in spite of myself towards scenes which I could not doubt were fearful; and I can boldly say that if Lawrence had hesitated to go I would have gone alone.

Taking the candle in my hand, then, I advanced at once towards the door. Lawrence stopped a moment to examine by the light I had left behind a pair of pistols which he had brought in his pockets.

Thus I had reached the door before he came up, and had opened it, for all the iron-work but a latch had been carried off.

The moment it was thrown back, the cries and groans were heard more distinctly than before; but I could see nothing before me but darkness, and it required a moment or two for the light to penetrate the darkness beyond. I had not taken two steps beyond the threshold ere Lawrence was by my side, and we found ourselves in a stone passage without windows, appearing to lead round the building. Ten paces on, however, we came to the top of a flight of steps, broken and mouldy, with grass and weeds growing up between the crevices. It was a work of some danger to descend those steps, for they rocked and tottered under the foot.

When we were about half-way down, the sounds, which had been growing louder and louder, suddenly ceased, and a death-like stillness succeeded.

'Stay a bit,' said my companion: 'let us reconnoitre. We may as well look before we leap. Hold up the light.'

I did as he asked, but the faint rays of the candle showed us nothing but the black irregular faces of the rock on either side, a small rill of water percolating through a crevice, and flowing over, down upon the steps, along which it poured in miniature cascades, and beyond, a black chasm where we could see nothing.

'Come on,' said Lawrence, advancing; 'we must see the end of it.'

Forward we went – down, down, some two-and-thirty steps more, without hearing another sound; but just as we reached the bottom step something gave a wild sort of yell, and I could hear a scrambling and tumbling at a good distance in advance.

My heart beat terribly, and Lawrence stopped short. I was far more agitated than he was, but he showed what he felt more, and anyone who had seen us would have said that he was frightened, I perfectly cool. He had passed me on the stairs; I now passed him, and holding the light high up gazed around.

It was very difficult to see anything distinctly, but here and there the beams caught upon rough points of rock, and low arches rudely hewn in the dark stone, and I made out that we were in a series of vaults excavated below the castle, with massive partitions between them, and here and there a doorway or passage from one to the other.

It seemed a perfect labyrinth at first sight, and now that all was silent again, we had nothing to guide us. I listened, but all was still as death; and I was advancing again, when my companion asked me to stop, and proposed that we should examine the ground on each side as we went on, marking the spot from which we started. It seemed a good plan, and I was stooping down to pile up some of the loose stones with which the ground or floor was plentifully encumbered, when a large black snake glided away, and at the same moment a bat or a small owl flitted by, and extinguished the light with its wings.

'Good Heaven, how unlucky!' cried Lawrence; 'have you got the match-box?'

'No,' I answered; 'I left it on the floor near where I was sleeping. Feel your way up the steps, my good friend, and bring it and the other candle. I will remain here till you come. Be quick!'

'You go; let me stay,' said Lawrence. But I was ashamed to accept his offer; and there was a something, I knew not what, that urged me to remain. 'No, no,' I said, 'go quickly; but give me one of your pistols,' and I repeated the last words in German, lest anyone who understood that language should be within earshot.

We were so near the foot of the steps that Lawrence could make no mistake, and I soon heard his feet ascending at a rapid rate, tripping and stumbling, it is true, but still going on. As I listened, I thought I heard a light sound also from the other side, but I concluded that it was but the echo of his steps through the hollow passages, and I stood quite still, hardly breathing. I could hear my heart beat, and the arteries of the throat were very unpleasant – throb, throb, throbbing.

After a moment or two I heard Lawrence's feet as it seemed to me almost above me, and I know not what impression of having some other being near me, made me resolve to cock the pistol. I tried to do it with my thumb as I held it in my right hand, but the lock went hard, and I found it would be necessary to lay down the candle to effect it.

Just as I was stooping to do so, I became suddenly conscious of having some living creature close by me; and the next instant I felt cold fingers at my throat, and an arm thrown round me. Not a word was spoken, but the grasp became tight upon my neck, and I struggled violently for breath and life. But the strength of the being that grasped me seemed gigantic, and his hand felt like a hand of iron.

Oh what a moment was that! Never, except in a terrible dream, have I felt anything like it. I tried to cry, to shout, but I could not, his hold of my throat was so tight; power of muscle seemed to fail me; my head turned giddy; my heart felt as if stopping; flashes of light shone from my eyes.

My right hand, however, was free, and by a violent effort I forced back the cock of the pistol nearly to the click; but then I lost all power. The hammer fell; the weapon went off with a loud echoing report, and for an instant, by the flash, I saw a hideous face with a grey beard close gazing into mine.

The sound of Lawrence's footsteps running rapidly over-head were the most joyful I had ever heard; but the next instant I felt myself cast violently backward, and I fell half stunned and bewildered to the ground.

Before I could rise the light of the candle began to appear, as Lawrence came down the stairs, first faint, and then brighter; and I heard his voice exclaiming, 'What has happened? what has happened?'

'Take care!' I cried faintly; 'there is some man or some devil here, and he has half killed me!'

Looking carefully around, Lawrence helped me to rise, and then we picked up the candle I had let fall and lighted it again, he gazing in my face from time to time, but seeming hardly to like to take his eyes off the vaults, or to enter into any conversation, for fear of some sudden attack. Nothing was to be seen, however; my savage assailant was gone, leaving no trace behind him but a cut upon the back of my head, received as he cast me backward.

'What has happened?' said Lawrence at length, in a very low voice. 'Why, your face looks quite blue, and you are bleeding!'

'No wonder,' I answered; 'for I have been half strangled, and have nearly had my brains dashed out.'

From time to time he asked a question, and I answered, till he had heard all that had happened, and then, after a minute's thought, he said, 'Do you know, I think we had better give this up, and barricade ourselves into the room upstairs. There may be more of these ruffians than one.'

'No, no,' I answered; 'I am resolved to see the end of it. There is only one, depend upon it, or I should have had both upon me. We are two, and can deal with him at all events. I have a great notion that some crime has been committed here this night, and we ought to ascertain the facts. Those first shrieks were from a woman's voice.'

'Well, well,' answered my companion, 'I am with you, if you are ready. Here, take one light and one pistol, and you examine the right-hand vaults while I take the left. We are now on our guard, and can help each other.'

We walked on accordingly, very slowly and carefully, taking care to look around us at every step, for the vaults were very rugged and irregular, and there was many a point and angle which might have concealed an assailant, but we met with no living creature. At length I thought I perceived a glimmer of light before me, but a little to the left, and calling up Lawrence, who was at some yard's distance, I pointed it out to him.

'To be sure I see it,' he answered; 'it is the moon shining. We must be near the entrance of the vaults. But what is that? There seems to be someone lying down there.'

He laid his hand upon my arm as he spoke, and we both stood still and gazed forward. The object towards which his eyes were directed certainly looked like a human figure, but it moved not in the least, and I slowly advanced towards it. Gradually I discerned what it was. There was the dress of a woman, gay coloured and considerably ornamented, and a neat little foot and shoe, with a small buckle in it, resting on a piece of fallen rock. The head was away from us, and she lay perfectly still.

My spirit felt chilled; but I went on, quickening my pace, and Lawrence and I soon stood beside her, holding the lights over her.

She was a young girl of nineteen or twenty, dressed in gala costume, with some touch of the city garb, some of the peasant attire. Her hair, which was all loose, wet, and dishevelled, was exceedingly rich and beautiful, and her face must have been very pretty in the sweet happy colouring of health and life. Now it was deathly pale, and the windows of the soul were closed. It was a sad, sad sight to see!

Her garments were all wet, and there was some froth about the mouth, but the fingers of the hands were limp and natural, as if there had been no struggle, and the features of the face were not distorted. There was, however, a wound upon her temple, from which some blood had flowed, and some scratches upon her cheek, and upon the small fair ears.

How came she by her death? How came she there? Was she slain by accident, or had she met with violence? were the questions that pressed upon our thoughts. But we said little then, and after a time left her where we found her. It mattered not to her that the bed was hard or the air cold.

We searched every corner of the vaults, however, for him I could not help believing her murderer, but without success; and on going to the mouth of the vault, where there had once been a door, long gone to warm some peasant's winter hearth, we found that it led out upon the road close by the side of the Rhine, and hardly a dozen paces from the river.

It was clear how he had escaped; and we sadly took our way back to the chamber above, where we passed the rest of the night in melancholy talk over the sad events that must have happened.

We slept no more, nor tried to sleep; but as soon as the east was grey went down to the shed where we had left the horses, and resumed our journey, to give information at the next village of what we had discovered.

The horses were very stiff, and at first could hardly drag us along, for the road was in a horrible state, but they soon warmed to the work, and in little more than three-quarters of an hour we reached a small village, where we got some refreshment, while the landlord of the little Gasthaus ran at my request for the Polizei.

When the only officer in the place came, I told him everything that had happened in the best German I could muster, and willingly agreed to go back with him to the spot, and show him where the body lay. The rumour spread like wildfire in the village; a crowd of the good peasantry collected round the door; and when we set out, taking a torch or two with us, as I described the vaults as very dark, we had at least a hundred persons in our train, among whom were a number of youths and young girls.

As nothing but one old chaise was to be procured in the village, and it did not look as if it would rain, we pursued our way on foot, but we certainly accomplished the distance faster than we had done with two horses in the morning. All the way the officer – I really do not know his right German title – continued conversing with Lawrence, who did not understand a word of German, and with myself, for whom his German was a world too fast.

I gave him, however, all the information I could, and as his language has the strange peculiarity of being easier to speak than to understand, I made him master, I believe, of every little incident of the last eventful night.

My description of the face of the man who had first nearly strangled me and then nearly dashed my brains out, and of whom I had caught a glimpse by the flash of the pistol, seemed to interest him more than all the rest. He stopped when I gave it to him, called several of the girls and young men about him, and conversed with them for a moment or two with a good deal of eagerness.

The greater part of what they said escaped me, but I heard a proper name frequently repeated, sounding like Herr Katzenberger, and the whole ended with a sad and gloomy shake of the head.

Soon after we resumed our advance we came to the mouth of the vault. It required no torches, however, to let us see what we sought for. The sun, still low, was shining slantingly beneath the heavy brows of the rocky arch, and the rays receded to the spot where the body of the poor girl lay.

They made a little bier of vine poles and branches, and laid the fair corpse upon it. Then they sought for various green leaves and some of the long-lingering autumn flowers, and strewed them tastefully over the body; and then four stout men raised the death-litter on their shoulders and bore it away towards the village.

I had the policeman for my companion; and beseeching him to speak slowly, I asked if he could give me any explanation of the strange and terrible events which must have happened.

'We know very little as yet,' he answered; 'but we shall probably know more soon. This young lady, poor thing! was the only daughter of a rich but cross-grained man, living at a village a short way further down the Rhine, on the other side. Her mother, who died three years ago, was from our own village. She was dancing away gaily last evening with our young folks, just before the storm came on; for her father had brought her up in his boat, and left her at her aunt's.

'When it came on with thunder and lightning, they all

went into the house, and, as misfortune would have it, that young lad who is carrying the head of the bier sat down by her in a corner, and they could not part soon enough. He was a lover of hers, everyone knew; but her father was hard against the match, and before they had been in the house an hour the old man came in and found them chatting in their corner. Perhaps he would have stayed all night had it not been for that; but he got very angry, and made her go away with him in his boat in the very midst of the storm.

'He said he had been on the Rhine many a worse night than that – though few of us had ever seen one. But he was obstinate as a bull, and away they went, though she cried terribly, both from fear and vexation. What happened after, none of us can tell, but old Herr Katzenberger has a grey beard, just such as you speak of.'

They carried the body to the little old church, and laid it in the aisle; and then they sent for the village doctor to examine into the mode of her death. I was not present when he came, but I heard afterward that he pronounced her to have died from drowning, and declared that the wound on the temple must have occurred by a blow against some rock when life was quite or nearly extinct. 'Otherwise,' he said, 'it would have bled much more, for the artery itself was torn.'

For my part, I was marched up with Lawrence to the Ampthaus, and there subjected to manifold interrogatories, the answers to which were all carefully taken down.

In the midst of these we were interrupted by the inroad of a dozen of peasants, dragging along a man who struggled violently with them, but in whom every one present recognised the father of the poor girl whose body we had found. The peasants said they had found him some six miles off, tearing his flesh with his teeth, and evidently in a state of furious insanity. They had found it very difficult to master him, they declared, for his strength was prodigious.

He was the only witness of what had taken place during that terrible night upon the river, and he could give no sane account. He often accused himself of murdering his child; but the good people charitably concluded that he merely meant he had been the cause of her death by taking her upon the treacherous waters on such a night as that; and the fact of his boat having drifted ashore some miles further down, broken and bottom upward, seemed to confirm that opinion.

I made some inquiries regarding the unfortunate man during a subsequent tour; but I only learned that he continued hopelessly insane, without a glimmer of returning reason.

The Forsaken of God

by William Mudford

The Scottish writer William Mudford (1782–1848) was born in Half Moon Street, Piccadilly, which, a century and a half later, was to be the setting of a famous horror story of stage and screen – The Man in Half Moon Street.

More prolific as a critic and translator than as an original story-teller, Mudford adapted from the French such works as The Life of Fenelon and The Memoirs of Prince Eugene of Savoy. His critical works include studies of Oliver Goldsmith, Doctor Johnson and James Bertie. Among his novels are The Five Nights of St Albans, a sixteenth century romance; The Premier (1831) and Stephen Dugard (1840). In addition, Mudford contributed many anonymous articles and stories to Blackwood's Edinburgh Magazine. The best known of these was The Iron Shroud (1832), a powerful tale of a condemned man's slow death that is not unlike something Poe might have written. It was quickly issued as a chapbook which proved enduringly profitable.

In language and subject, The Forsaken of God, selected from Tales and Trifles, a posthumous collection of 1849, ably demonstrates that the spirit of the Gothic Terror Tale had not yet been laid.

'FOR Heaven's sake! Frederick, do not go,' exclaimed the terrified Adolphine, holding her brother by the arm to detain him.

'Why not?' replied Frederick. 'If Hermann can do *his* part, I'll be sworn to go through mine.'

' 'Tis unholy! 'tis hellish! 'tis an impious daring of the Almighty! and you shall *not* go,' said Adolphine. 'My blood curdles at my heart to *think* only of what you have said!'

'Why, look you, Adolphine,' answered Frederick, laughing, as he disengaged himself gently from the clinging arms of his sister; 'what is it after all? Hermann says he can raise the dead; and I say, if he can, I am he that will hold a parley with the dead; a conference such as living man ne'er yet had.'

'Oh, God!' exclaimed Adolphine, covering her eyes with her hands, and shuddering as she spoke, 'the bare imagination of it is horrible.'

'Shall I tell you a secret?' continued Frederick. 'I believe Hermann less able to perform his part than mine.'

'Still, it is sinful mockery – if it be only mockery,' said Adolphine.

The deep heavy bell of the cathedral struck eleven. Frederick starting up, threw his cloak round him, put on his hat, and prepared to quit the house.

'I have not a moment to play with now,' said he. 'Hermann expects me before twelve, and it is a long walk to where he lives.'

'Do not, do not go!' exclaimed Adolphine, in a tone of earnest supplication, as she once more flung herself upon his bosom to detain him.

'By my faith, but I must. If Hermann has spoken truly, he has ere this gone through pains and torments, to vex the graves which are to yield up their pale inhabitants for my pleasure, that I dare not trifle with. Besides, would he not ever after despise me as a coward, big of speech, but faint of resolution, should I leave to him the boast of having prepared a scene which I was too sick at heart to look upon? To-morrow, with the dawn, I shall return; and then, Adolphine –'

'And then, it will be time to tell her more, thou loitering babbler,' exclaimed a voice, whose freezing breath fell upon the ear of Frederick like an icy current of keen winter air. He alone heard it. He started and shivered at the mysterious rebuke. The next moment he was on his way to Hermann's dwelling in the mountains, and Adolphine was on her knees, praying fervently for his safety.

Hermann and Frederick were fellow students in one of the German universities. It matters little what one; as little, when the compact we are describing was made; whether a century or two centuries ago. It *was* made – for its history is extant. Hermann, who was older by some years than Frederick, was reputed to be deeply skilled in the lore of necromancy and magic, and to have acquired the fearful power of controlling the spirits of darkness, so as to make them work his will. Whether he really possessed this power, no one knew, though every one asserted it, and Hermann himself did not deny it.

It chanced on one occasion, when he and Frederick were walking through a churchyard, the latter, who delighted in strange, wild fancies, observed, as he paused to survey the tombs around them, 'If a man now could bid these graves yawn, and cast forth their dead, to be questioned of what they once were, and what they are, and they constrained to answer truly whatsoever might be demanded of them – God of Heaven! what marvellous secrets we should learn!'

'As how?' inquired Hermann.

'Oh! think ye not that we should find innocence that had bled upon the scaffold, for unacted crimes? Murder, and sacrilege, and robbery, and sin of every kind, dying on beds of down, cozening to the last all but Heaven and a howling conscience? Should we not see hearts broken by secret griefs, that never were told to mortal ears? Fathers and mothers killed by their unnatural children? – the young and beautiful withered by love's perjuries? poison and steel shortening the years that lay between heirs and their inheritance? And all these undiscovered villainies smuggled out of the world, with certificates of old age – consumption – apoplexy – from grave physicians who take fees to give names to what they cannot cure.'

Hermann mused in silence.

'Here,' continued Frederick, planting his foot upon a new-made grave – 'here lies one who but yesterday was laid in the earth perhaps. Imagine I could say to him or her arise – that I could call back speech and memory to the dull clod – that I could hold in my hand, as a book, the heart that has ceased to throb. Should I not read there something which the world had never read, during all the long years it dwelt in it?'

' 'Tis an odd fancy, Frederick,' exclaimed Hermann; 'a very odd fancy. Since when has such a notion possessed you?'

'Since my mother died,' replied Frederick emphatically.

'And she died – '

'Oh, ask the doctor. He'll tell you 'twas of atrophy, and prove it by his art. I laughed amid my tears to hear them talk; and then it was I first thought how the dead would answer for themselves.'

'Let us go,' said Hermann, and they quitted the church-yard.

Many times afterwards the two friends discoursed upon this theme, which Hermann could not banish from his thoughts; and one evening, when they were passing through this same churchyard, he thus addressed Frederick:

'Do you remember,' said he, 'our conversation here, some months ago?'

'I do; and our frequent ones since.'

'*I* can perform the thing you wish.'

'Would you were able!' answered Frederick.

'I can do it.'

'What?'

'Lay open these graves!'

'Pooh!' exclaimed Frederick laughing. 'Come along, Hermann; you are making sport of me.'

'Hear me,' said Hermann, remaining fixed to the spot where he stood. 'I am not, as you imagine, merrily disposed; but I mean to use no persuasion – no argument with you. Simply, and in plain words, I repeat, I can lay these graves open, and command the dust and ashes they contain to take forms of life: even the very shapes they bore when living.'

'Thou canst do this?'

'This, and more. They shall reveal to you those marvellous secrets you spoke of.'

'Hermann!' exclaimed Frederick, looking at his friend with an eye that flashed horrible delight. 'Hermann! swear that you will do this; swear, by some oath, terrible as the thing itself, and I will pawn my soul to the eternal enemy of man for the pledge of my part in it.'

'There needs nor oath nor plight to bind the willing and the bold. I am the first; are *you* the second?'

'Here is my hand. When shall it be?' replied Frederick.

'We will settle that as we walk along,' answered Hermann.

They did settle it; and the night was now come in which Frederick was to be convinced (for he doubted to the last) whether Hermann could really perform this fearful feat of sorcery. He arrived at his house later than the time appointed, in consequence of the delay occasioned by Adolphine's entreaties to forego the meeting altogether; and Hermann was looking out for him. He returned to his room, followed by Frederick.

'I had worked for nothing,' said he, angrily, 'had I not gone beyond the need of this night's labour, to break the spell of a fond girl. Are these matters that women should know? Adolphine is on her knees still, and her prayers have a holiness in them that thwarts and disturbs my purpose. But I can perform – I can perform!' he muttered to himself as he rolled something in the palms of his hands that emitted sparks of a crimson hue, with a loud crackling. 'I can – ha! bravely! bravely!' and he increased the rolling motion of his hands; 'her eyes close – her head droops – 'tis a sound sleep: it will last till the lark sings.'

As he uttered these words, his hands unclosed; the palms were of a deep, blood-red colour, but there was no visible appearance of any substance that had been rubbed between them.

Frederick remembered the freezing voice that had rebuked him, and no longer doubted of Hermann's power. If he could thus hold communion with the living, why might not the dead be subject to his art?

The room was lighted by a single taper, which burned thick and duskily. On a table in the middle of it lay several open books, traced with strange characters, and encircled with the skeletons of birds, reptiles, and animals. The appearance of Hermann himself was so strangely altered that Frederick could scarcely recognise him. His face was pallid even to ghastliness; his arms were naked to the elbow; his long black hair knotted; and his tall gaunt figure enveloped in a robe made from the skin of a leopard. The girdle by which it was fastened looked like twisted snakes, for there was a constant heaving and writhing of it about his body.

Frederick noted these things while Hermann was speaking. When he ceased, he said, with an air of gaiety,

'I like your dress vastly, Hermann; 'tis excellent masquerade; but am not I too, to be equipped for this great occasion?'

'*There* hangs thy robe,' replied Hermann, pointing with his finger.

Frederick started. Was it Hermann that had spoken? or was it a voice creaked from the bony lungs of death himself? He turned round in the direction of the pointed finger. Again he started recoiling several paces. – An arm – an arm merely – joined to no body, was extended behind him, holding a winding sheet. The flesh was upon it, but livid and in corruption: and there it hung, suspended in mid air, balanced and supported he knew not how, offering him a shroud that had the soil of the grave upon it!

'There needs nor oath nor plight to bind the willing and the bold,' said Hermann, in the same unearthly tone. 'I am the first: art thou the second?'

'Ay!' responded Frederick; 'thou hast my word, Hermann; but – '

' 'Tis past questioning now,' interrupted Hermann. 'The dead are waiting for us, and we *must* go. Quick, quick; clothe thyself.'

Frederick rallied from his trepidation, and advancing with a resolute step, plucked the winding sheet from the spectre hand. At the same moment there was heard a low wailing sound, which continued till he had folded round his creeping flesh the sepulchral garment.

The horrible half-decayed arm remained. Hermann drew from his bosom a charmed glove, woven of the down that lines the screech-owl's wings. He gave it to Frederick.

'*That* must with us,' said he, pointing to the arm; 'but at the touch of living flesh it would dissolve to putrid jelly. Put on this; grasp it boldly; and all is done till we stand in the churchyard.'

Frederick did as he was commanded without uttering a word. He put on the charmed glove; he grasped the arm. It had substance; it was heavy; and so chilling cold that it benumbed his own, as if it were solid ice. His teeth chattered; his body shook; the shroud struck a freezing shudder through his veins; and this seemed to heighten it. He looked at Hermann. He would have spoken, but his lips were rigid; as unapt for motion as the marble lips of a statue.

'From this moment until sunrise,' said Hermann, 'you have no power to exchange thoughts but with the dead. You hunger for their secrets; but know you not that the grave is a curtain dropped between two worlds? He who uplifts it, cannot be of both, save at the price you have to pay. Come!'

Frederick heard this terrible denunciation with an appalled spirit. He determined to renounce his design. He strove to fling the arm from him. – It clung to his hand, as if it had been riveted there with clasps of iron. He endeavoured to tear off the shroud. It seemed to have grown to him; and that it would have been as easy to wrench away his limbs.

Hermann laughed aloud as he repeated Frederick's own words: 'Swear that you will do this – swear by some oath terrible as the thing itself, and I will pawn my soul to the eternal enemy of man for the pledge of my part in it!' – 'Saidst thou not so? And dost thou quail already? Summon all that's man in thee for what remains. Come! They who wait for us will grow impatient.'

Hermann led the way; Frederick followed with a staggering step. The night was preternaturally dark; it appeared as if they were walking under a thick canopy of black mist, which veiled the heavens from their sight. The path that Hermann took was through the tangled alleys of the forest; a nearer, but more difficult road to the churchyard. He talked, sung, laughed, and acted, the whole way the part of a man whose spirits were elated by the prospect of a festal meeting. He jeered Frederick ironically upon what he called, 'his dogged silence': the forest rang with his laughter at every stumble he made; and he bade him note how nimbly he threaded the narrow paths, though he had nor more nor better eyes than himself. Frederick listened to him with feelings which it were impossible to describe. It was not Hermann he was following – he was sure it was not Hermann – it was some fiend, in Hermann's shape, for Hermann was grave, austere, melancholy – never given to gamesome moods; and least of all could Hermann, his friend, his brother almost, exult so *like* a fiend in the agony of mind he was enduring.

They stand beside a grave. Hermann sprinkles upon it a powder, which falls in sparkles of light from his fingers. The earth begins to heave; and presently, as a volcano casts up its ashes, the grave empties itself. Slowly and slowly, like the rippling waves of a becalmed ocean, it rises to the surface, divides, and falls in crumbling heaps on either side. Then there ascends the venerable figure of an aged man, clothed in robes of purple and scarlet, the ensigns of senatorial dignity. At the same moment, the spectre arm, by wondrous motion of its own, tears itself aloft, and becomes a dimly gleaming torch; each livid finger sending forth pale red dusky flames, which fling a horrid glare upon the cadaverous features of the phantom.

'I cannot hold him longer than while thy quickened pulse shall beat a hundred,' said Hermann in a whisper. 'In that space thou must master what secrets thou would'st learn.'

'I know thee!' exclaimed Frederick, with a faltering voice, 'thou wert the traitor, Wulfstein, who conspired against thy prince's life! I saw the headsman execute justice on thee, thou, to the last, calling Heaven to witness thy innocence: but all men knew thee guilty.'

'*One* man knew I was not,' said the phantom; and a grim smile grew upon his corpse-like face.

'And he – ,' rejoined Frederick.

'Shall I name him?'

'Aye – '

' 'TWAS THY FATHER! Most foully he shed *my* blood to save his own!'

The phantom vanished – the grave closed – the pale-red dusky flames of the unhallowed torch expired – a yell of exulting voices, as if the fiends of the abyss were triumphing, sounded in the air – and Frederick was again mute. Hermann clapped him on the shoulder, exclaiming, in a tone of taunting bitterness, 'Rare secrets! brave secrets! marvellous revelations for the living!'

They stand beside a second grave. The same ceremonies – the same effects: the earth heaves, the sepulchre yawns, the torch of the charnel-house uprears itself, and burns. The resemblance of a fair beautiful youth, with radiant eyes and clustering locks, stands before them.

'I know *thee*, too!' exclaimed Frederick striving in vain to draw down his arm, so that the lurid flame might not gleam upon the shape – 'My brother!'

'Who died by a brother's hand!'

'But I was guiltless – I was guiltless, dear Francis!' rejoined Frederick, in a tone of piercing anguish. 'My arrow flew at the fierce wolf, when thou, crossing its path, received it in thy heart!'

'Did I upbraid thee for my death, as that heart's blood fell upon thee? Were not my words words of consolation? Strove I not to soothe the pangs with which that blameless deed of slaughter filled thee?'

'Thou didst – thou didst! Avaunt! Hide thee from mine eyes, or I shall grow mad. Oh! I sought not *this*!'

'Think of the wretched misery our mother bore, whilst

thou whole days and nights didst suffer her to mourn, in ignorance, my loss! Think what a stain, even to this hour, lies upon the innocent name of one who lives dishonoured in the suspicion of *thy* act! Thou canst not redeem the past: but thou mayst make the future witness of thy tardy justice.'

Frederick had covered his eyes with his hand, unable to look upon this vision. When he withdrew his hand it was gone. They were again in silence and darkness; but he heard the voice of Hermann at his side, in the same tone of taunting bitterness, repeating his own words: 'Thou saidst truly, my friend. Thou hast now "read something, which the world never read". Oh, these dead! "how they answer for themselves", Frederick! 'Tis rare sport to bid them thus arise – to "call back speech and memory to the dull clods" – to "hold their hearts in our hands, and peruse them as a book!" Truth is not of this world; and they were fools who looked for her in the bottom of a well; her temple is the grave! her oracles, dust and ashes!'

The scene was changed. They stood beneath the ruined porch of the church. The doors flew open with a rattling sound; they entered: the vast edifice was wrapped in impenetrable gloom, except the little circle of dismal light from the horrible torch. They advanced to the altar, the steps of which Hermann ascended alone, silently motioning his companion to remain. He waved his hands over the tall wax tapers that stood upon the table of the altar, when, by some strange spell, blue forked flames descended upon them, and they burned with dim ghastly flashes that shot forth each moment. By this fitful glare Frederick could perceive all he did and all he looked; for this aspect was now wild, terrific, demon-like.

He took the sacramental chalice, and stretching forth his bare arm, cried in a loud voice, 'Come ye viewless ministers of this dread hour! come from the fenny lake, the hanging rock, and the midnight cave! The moon is red – the stars are out – the sky is burning – and all nature stands aghast at what we do!' Then replacing the sacred vessel on the altar, he drew, one by one, from different parts of his body, from his knotted hair, from his bosom, from beneath his nails, the unholy things which he cast into it.

'This,' said he, 'I plucked from the beak of a raven feeding on a murderer's brains! This is the mad dog's foam! These the spurgings of a dead man's eyes, gathered since the rising of the evening star! This is a screech-owl's egg! This a single drop of black blood, squeezed from the heart of a sweltered toad! This, an adder's tongue! And here, ten grains of the gray moss that grew upon a skull which had lain in the charnel-house three hundred years! What! not yet?' And his eyes seemed like balls of fire as he cast them upwards. 'Not yet? I call ye once! I call ye twice! Dare ye deny me! Nay, then, as I call ye thrice, I'll wound mine arm, and as it drops, I'll breathe a spell shall cleave the ground and drag you here!'

He held his left arm over the chalice, clutched it with his hand, and as if the talons of an eagle had infixed themselves, the blood spouted forth. While it dripped into the vessel he gasped for breath like a strong man fighting hard with his last agonies.

Suddenly the tapers were extinguished, and there remained only the fearful glare that flickered horribly from the unhallowed torch. It reached not to the altar; so Frederick saw not Hermann. But he was upon its lowest step – HIS MOTHER! even as he had seen her the day he returned without his brother, when he spoke not the word that would have spared those long hours of grief which the mystery of his absence caused; to be followed, at last, by all a mother's heart could feel for the untimely death of a beloved son. He bent his knee in reverential awe before the sacred shade; and his soul grew faint within him; for there was upon that maternal face a sad look of pity and of wrath. He had thoughts that burned for utterance, but he had no tongue to give them utterance. The form spoke:

'Why hast thou troubled me in death, my son? Why hast thou in life arrayed thee in that garb of death? Why has thou disturbed MY sepulchre, for the shroud that infolds thee?'

A shriek of horror burst from him, as again he strove, but vainly, to tear off the sacrilegious spoil of his mother's grave.

'Son, thou hast sought, unholily, the secrets of the dead; hear MINE! The canker that preyed upon my life, was grief for thee. The forsaken of God are they alone who forsake God. All sinners else may hope to be partakers of his infinite mercies. THOU WERT GOD-FORSAKEN! Thou clothedst thyself in the pride of thy understanding – said there was NO GOD – and lived as if thou didst believe in thy impiety. I loved thee, for I bare thee – thou wert my child; but the thorns planted in my heart by the knowledge that my child must perish eternally, wounded it to death!'

The shadow faded away, and again the yell of exulting voices sounded in the ears of Frederick, as he lay prostrate on the cold damp pavement, shedding involuntary tears. They fell from his eyes like drops of molten lead. His brain seemed on fire. He groaned, and howled, and gnashed his teeth, and dashed his face furiously against the stones. He heard the voice of Hermann. Oh! the damning chuckle of that voice, as he jealously shouted – ' "Rare secrets! brave secrets! marvellous revelations for the living!" "Since when hath such a notion possessed you?" "Since my mother died!" "And she died – ?" "Oh ask the doctor," ha! ha! ha! "he'll tell you 'twas of atrophy;" ha! ha! ha! "I laughed amid my tears to hear them talk; and then it was that I first thought how the dead would answer for themselves." Ha! ha! ha! Laugh, man, laugh as I do! Laugh NOW, amid thy tears, thou desperate fool!'

The next morning, Frederick was found a corpse in the abbey church, at the foot of his mother's tomb, leading to the altar. Adolphine told what she knew of the compact between him and Hermann; but Hermann brought forward two fellow students with whom he had passed the preceding evening; and his own servant proved that he retired to bed at eleven, where he found him at the usual hour when he went to call him. Hermann himself, too, denied that he had ever entered into such a compact; wept for the death of his friend, and triumphed over his accusers. Yet, had he been required to bare his left arm, there would have appeared upon it the fresh blood marks of lacerated flesh, as if torn by an eagle's talons!

The Monk's Story

by Catherine Crowe

*Of all the Victorian ladies who undertook to write supernatural
stories, none was better equipped for the task, emotionally and
intellectually, than Mrs Catherine Crowe (1800–1876). A disciple
of the Scottish phrenologist George Combe, Mrs Crowe was an ardent
student of spiritualism and the twilight zone of human behaviour,
the study of which we now call psychology. Apart from* Light and
Darkness *(1850), from which this story is taken, Mrs Crowe
produced several non-fiction works of occultism –* Ghosts and Family
Legends, Spiritualism and the Age We Live In *and the
influential* Night Side of Nature. *And in 1845 she translated
into English* The Seeress of Prevost *by the German natural
scientist Justinius Kerner.*

*It is interesting to note how, as in this instance, the supernatural
tale merged with the so-called domestic story of middle-class life
(Mrs Crowe also wrote domestic stories, the most successful being*
Susan Hopely, or the Adventures of a Maid Servant *(1841).
Monks were still a necessary ingredient but whereas the Gothic
fictions of 'Monk' Lewis and Horace Walpole took place in what
might be termed 'Utopias of the Horrid', by the time Mrs Crowe was
writing the horrors were much closer to real life, happening to perfectly
respectable young men such as one invited to dinner.*

*Montague Summers, whose knowledge of the occult and its
literature was encyclopaedic, noted that* The Monk's Story *was
'admirably told and little less than a masterpiece of its kind.'*

CHAPTER I

ONE evening on which a merry Christmas party was assembled in an hospitable country mansion in the north of England, one of the company, a young man named Charles Lisle, called the host aside, as they were standing in the drawing-room before dinner, and whispered, 'I say, Graham, I wish you'd put me into a room that has either a bolt or a key.'

'They have all keys, or should have,' returned Mr Graham.

'The key of my room is lost,' returned the other. 'I asked the housemaid. It is always the first thing I look to when I enter a strange bed-chamber. I can't sleep unless the door is locked.'

'How very odd! I never locked my door in my life,' said Mr Graham. 'I say, Letitia,' continued he, addressing his wife, 'here's Charlie Lisle can't sleep unless his door's locked, and the room you've put him into has no key.'

At this announcement all the ladies looked with surprise at Charlie Lisle, and all the gentlemen laughed; and 'how odd!' and 'what a strange fancy!' was echoed among them.

'I daresay you think it very odd, and indeed it must appear rather a lady-like particularity,' responded Lisle, who was a fine active young man, and did not look as if he were much troubled with superfluous fears; 'but a circumstance that occurred to me when I was on the continent last summer has given me a nervous horror of sleeping in a room with an unlocked door, and I have never been able to overcome it. This is perhaps owing to my having been ill at the time, and I can scarcely say I have recovered from the effects of that illness yet.'

Naturally, everybody wanted to hear what this adventure was – the programme being certainly exciting – and so one of the visitors offered to exchange rooms with Charlie Lisle, provided he would tell them his story; which accordingly, when assembled round the fire in the evening, he began in the following words:—

'You must know, then, that last year, when I was wandering over the continent partly in search of the picturesque, and partly to remedy the effects of too much study, or rather too hasty study – for I believe a man may study as much as he pleases, if he will only take it easy, as the Irish say – I was surprised one evening by a violent storm of hail, and it became so suddenly dark, that I could scarcely see my horse's head. I had twelve miles to go to the town at which I intended to pass the night, and I knew that there was no desirable shelter nearer, unless I chose to throw myself on the hospitality of the monastery of Pierre Châtel, which lay embosomed amongst the hills a little to the east of the road I was travelling. There is something romantic and interesting in a residence at a convent, but of that I need not now say anything. After a short mental debate, I resolved to present myself at the convent gate, and ask them to give me a night's shelter. So I turned off the road, and rang the heavy bell, which was answered by a burly, rosy-cheeked lay brother, and he forthwith conducted me to the Prior, who was called the Père Jolivet. He received me very kindly, and we chatted away for some time on politics and the affairs of the world; and when the brothers were summoned to the refectory, I begged leave to join them, and share their simple repast, instead of eating the solitary supper prepared for me.

'There were two tables in the hall, and I was seated next the Prior, in a situation that gave me a pretty good view of the whole company; and as I cast my eyes round to take a survey of the various countenances, they were suddenly arrested by one that struck me as about the most remarkable I had ever beheld. From the height of its owner as he sat, I judged he must be a very tall man, and the high round shoulders gave an idea of great physical strength; though at the same time the whole mass seemed composed of bone, for there was very little muscle to cover it. The colour of his great coarse face was of an unnatural whiteness, and the rigid immobility of his features favoured the idea that the man was more dead than alive. There was altogether something so remarkable in his looks, that I could with difficulty turn my eyes from him. My fixed gaze, I imagine, roused some emotions within him, for he returned my scrutiny with a determined and terrific glare. If I forced myself to turn away my head for a moment, round it would come again, and there were his two great mysterious eyes upon me; and that stiff jaw, slowly and mechanically moving from side to side, as he ate his supper, like something acted on by a pendulum. It was really dreadful: we seemed both bewitched to stare at each other; and I longed for the signal to rise, that I might be released from the strange fascination. This came at length; and though I had promised myself to make some inquiries of the Prior concerning the owner of the eyes, yet not finding myself alone with him during the evening, I forbore, and in due time retired to my chamber, intending to proceed on my journey the following day. But when the morning came, I found myself very unwell, and the hospitable Prior recommended me not to leave my bed; and finally, I was obliged to remain there not only that day, but many days; in short, it was nearly a month before I was well enough to quit the convent.

'In the meantime, however, I had learnt the story of Brother Lazarus, for so I found the object of my curiosity was called; and had thereby acquired some idea of the kind of influence he had exercised over me. The window of the little room I occupied looked into the burying-place of the monastery; and on the day I first left my bed, I perceived a monk below digging a grave. He was stooping forward, with his spade in his hand, and with his back towards me; and as my room was a good way from the ground, and the brothers were all habited alike, I could not distinguish which of them it was.

' "You have a death amongst you?" said I to the Prior when he visited me.

' "No," returned he; "we have even no serious sickness at present."

' "I see one of the brothers below, digging a grave," I replied.

' "Oh!" said he, looking out, "that is Brother Lazarus – he is digging his own grave."

' "What an extraordinary fancy!" said I. "But perhaps it's a penance?"

' "Not a penance imposed by me," replied the Prior, "but by himself. Brother Lazarus is a very strange person. Perhaps you may have observed him at the refectory – he sat nearly opposite you at the other table?"

' "Bless me! is that he? Oh, yes, I observed him indeed. Who could help observing him? He has the most extraordinary countenance I ever beheld."

' "Brother Lazarus is a somnambulist," returned the Prior; "a natural somnambulist; and is altogether, as I said before, a very extraordinary character."

' "What!" said I, my curiosity being a good deal awakened, "does he walk in his sleep? I never saw a somnambulist before, and should like to hear some particulars about him, if you have no objection to tell them me."

' "They are not desirable inmates, I assure you," answered the Prior. "I could tell you some very odd adventures connected with this disease of Brother Lazarus."

' "I should be very much obliged to you, if you would," said I, with no little eagerness.

' "Somnambulists are sometimes subject to strange hallucinations," he replied; "their dream is to them as real as our actual daily life is to us, and they not unfrequently act out the scenes of the drama with a terrible determination. I will just give you one instance of the danger that may accrue from a delusion of this nature. At the last monastery I inhabited, before I became Prior of Pierre Châtel, we had a monk who was known to be a somnambulist. He was a man of a sombre character and gloomy temperament; but it was rather supposed that his melancholy proceeded from physical causes, than from any particular source of mental uneasiness. His nightly wanderings were very irregular: sometimes they were frequent, sometimes there were long intermissions.

Occasionally he would leave his cell, and after being absent from it several hours, would return of his own accord, still fast asleep, and lay himself in his bed: at other times he would wander so far away, that we had to send in search of him; and sometimes he would be met by the messengers on his way back, either awake or asleep, as it might happen.

' "This strange malady had caused us some anxiety, and we had not neglected to seek the best advice we could obtain with respect to its treatment; and at length the remedies applied seemed to have taken effect; the paroxysms became more rare, and the disease so far subsided, that it ceased to be a subject of observation amongst us. Several months had elapsed since I had heard anything of the nocturnal excursions of Brother Dominique, when one night that I had some business of importance in hand, instead of going to bed when the rest of the brotherhood retired to their cells, I seated myself at my desk, for the purpose of reading and answering certain letters concerning the affair in question. I had been some time thus occupied, and had just finished my work, and had already locked my desk preparatory to going to bed, when I heard the closing of a distant door, and immediately afterwards a foot in the long gallery that separated my room from the cells of the brotherhood. What could be the matter? Somebody must be ill, and was coming to seek assistance; and I was confirmed in this persuasion when I perceived that the foot was approaching my door, the key of which I had not turned. In a moment more it opened, and Fra Dominique entered, asleep. His eyes were wide open, but there was evidently no speculation in them; they were fixed and glassy, like the eyes of a corpse. He had nothing on but the tunic which he was in the habit of wearing at night, and in his hand he held a large knife. At this strange apparition I stood transfixed. From the cautious manner in which he had opened the door, and the stealthy pace with which he advanced into the room, I could not doubt that he was bent upon mischief; but aware of the dangerous effects that frequently result from the too sudden awakening of a sleep-walker, I thought it better to watch in silence the acting out of this fearful drama, than venture to disturb him. With all the precautions he would have used not to arouse me had he been awake, he moved towards the bed, and in so doing he had occasion to pass quite close to where I stood, and as the light of the lamps fell upon his face, I saw that his brows were knit, and his features contracted into an expression of resolute malignity. When he reached the bed, he bent over it, felt with his hand in the place where I should have been, and then, apparently satisfied, he lifted up his arm, and struck successively three heavy blows – so heavy, that, having pierced the bed-clothes, the blade of the knife entered far into the mattress, or rather into the mat that served me for one. Suddenly, however, whilst his arm was raised for another blow, he started, and turning round, hastened towards the window, which he opened, and had it been large enough, I think would have thrown himself out. But finding the aperture too small, he changed his direction. Again he passed close to me, and I felt myself shrink back as he almost touched me with his tunic. The two lamps that stood on my table made no impression on his eyes; he opened and closed the door as before; and I heard him proceed rapidly along the gallery, and retire to his own cell. It would be vain to attempt to describe the amazement with which I had witnessed this terrible scene. I had been, as it were, the spectator of my own murder, and I was overcome by the horrors of this visionary assassination. Grateful to Providence for the danger I had escaped, I yet could not brace my nerves to look at it with calmness, and I passed the remainder of the night in a state of painful agitation. On the following morning, as soon as breakfast was over, I summoned Fra Dominique to my room. As he entered, I saw his eye glance at the bed, which was now, however, covered by other linen, so that there were no traces visible of his nocturnal visit. His countenance was sad, but expressed no confusion, till I inquired what had been the subject of his dreams the preceding night. Then he started, and changed colour.

' "Reverend father," said he, "why do you ask me this?"

' "Never mind," said I; "I have my reasons."

' "I do not like to repeat my dream," returned he; "it was too frightful; and I fear that it must have been Satan himself that inspired it."

' "Nevertheless let me hear it."

' "Well, reverend father, if you will have it so, what I dreamt was this – but that you may the better comprehend my dream, I must give you a short sketch of the circumstances in which it originated."

' "Do so," said I; "and that we may not be interrupted, I'll lock the door." So having turned the key, and bade him seat himself on a stool opposite me, I prepared to listen to the story of his life.

CHAPTER II

' "I was a child," said he, "of eight years old when the event occurred in which my unhappy malady originated. My father had died, leaving my mother in tolerable circumstances and with two children, myself and a sister of marriageable years. This sister, as I have since understood, had become attached to an Italian stranger of very questionable character who had appeared in the town we inhabited, under the character of an itinerant artist. My father had discovered the connection, and had forbidden him the house; but when he died, the stranger's influence prevailed over my mother's authority, and one morning Adèle was missing. As the Italian disappeared at the same time, no doubt was entertained that they had gone off together, and a few weeks confirmed these apprehensions. They came back, declaring themselves married, and petitioning my mother's forgiveness and assistance. She granted them both; but finding her so easy to deal with, Ripa, the Italian, began to make such frequent demands upon her purse, and indulged in such violence when his drafts were not responded to, that she found it necessary to forbid him the house. I believe he had some talent, but he was idle and dissipated, and the habit of living upon us had so far augmented these vices, that he could no longer bring himself to work. The consequence was, that he soon fell into distress, and, finding my mother, whose resolution was sustained by her brother, inexorable, he had recourse to more desperate means of supplying his necessities. Many evil reports were circulated about him, and, at length, so much suspicion was excited, that, to my mother's great relief, they quitted the place, and several months elapsed without any tidings of their proceedings reaching her.

' "For my part, with the usual volatility of childhood, I had totally ceased to think either of Ripa or of my sister, of whom I had formerly been exceedingly fond, and I was wholly occupied with the prospect of going to school, a prospect which, as I had no companions of my own age at home, delighted me. My mother, on the contrary, suffered considerably from the idea of the impending separation; and the last night I was to sleep under her roof, she took me to lie in her bed.

' " 'I cannot part with you tonight, my child!' said she, as she kissed me, and led me to her chamber. 'You don't know what parting is yet, Dominique. You think only of the playfellows you are going to; you know not what you are about to lose!'

' "Little I dreamt of all I was going to lose, – nor she either.

' "I suppose I fell asleep directly, for I have no recollection of my mother's coming to bed, nor of anything else, till I was awakened by the pressure of a heavy hand on my breast, and, by the faint light of a lantern which stood on a table, I discovered my brother-in-law, Ripa, the Italian, hanging over me. But it was not at me he was looking, but at my mother, who, fast asleep, was lying on the other side of the bed. An instinctive terror kept me silent and motionless; and presently, having ascertained the position in which his victim was lying, he raised a large knife he held in his hand, and struck it repeatedly into her breast. At the third blow, my horror and anguish overcame my fears, and I uttered a cry which seems first to have revealed to him my presence; or perhaps he did not know it was me, but was only startled by the sudden noise, for, as his purpose was undoubtedly robbery, I do not see why he should not have despatched so insignificant an obstacle, and fulfilled his intentions. However this may be, he took fright and fled, first to the window, – for he seemed to have lost all presence of mind, – but finding no egress there, he turned and retreated by the door.

' "I was afraid he would return, and, almost dead with terror and grief, I lay still the rest of the night, without courage to rise, or to call the servant who slept in the kitchen. When she entered the room in the morning, she found my mother dead, and myself bathed in her blood. Ripa was pursued and taken, my testimony was fatal to him, and my poor sister died of a broken heart a few months after he had expiated his crime on the scaffold.

' "A long and fearful malady was the consequence to me of this dreadful event, and I have ever since been subject to these dreams!"

' "What dreams?" I asked.

' "Such as I had last night," he answered; "wherein I feel myself constrained to act over again the frightful scene I witnessed."

' "And pray," I inquired, "do you select any particular person as your victim in those dreams?"

' "Always."

' "And what does this selection depend upon? Is it enmity?"

' "No," returned Dominique; "it is a peculiar influence that I cannot explain. Perhaps," added he, after some hesitation, "you may have observed my eyes frequently fixed on you of late?" I remembered that I had observed this; and he then told me that whoever he looked at in that manner was the person he dreamt of.

'Such,' said Charlie Lisle, 'was the Prior's account of this strange personage. I confess, when I had heard his explanation, I began to feel particularly queer, for I was already satisfied that Fra Dominique and Brother Lazarus were one and the same person; and I perceived that I was in considerable danger of being the selected victim of his next dream; and so I told Père Jolivet.

' "Never fear," said he; "we lock him up every night, and have done so ever since my adventure. Added to which, he is now very unwell; he was taken with a fit yesterday, and we have been obliged to bleed him."

' "But he is digging there below," said I.

' "Yes," replied the Prior; "he has a notion he is going to die, and entreated permission to prepare his grave. It is, however, a mere fancy I daresay. He had the same notion during the indisposition that succeeded the dream I have just related. I forgot to tell you, however, though you seem to have penetrated the secret, that this Fra Dominique changed his name to Lazarus when he accompanied me here, which he was allowed to do at his own urgent entreaty; why, I cannot tell, but ever after that conversation, he seemed to have imbibed a strong attachment to me; perhaps because I exhibited none of the distrust or aversion towards him which some persons might have been apt to entertain under the same circumstances."

'A week after this I was informed that Brother Lazarus was dead,' continued Lisle; 'and I confess I did not much regret his decease. I thought a man subject to such dangerous dreams was better out of the world than in it; more especially as by all account he had no enjoyment in life. On the day I quitted the monastery, I saw from my window one of the brothers completing the already partly-made grave, and learnt that he was to be buried that evening; and as I descended the stairs, I passed some monks who were carrying his coffin to his cell. "Rest his soul!" said I, as I buckled on my spurs; and having heartily thanked the good prior for his hospitality, I mounted my horse and rode away.'

Here Charlie Lisle rang the bell and asked for a glass of water.

'Is that all?' inquired Lady Araminta.

'Not quite,' said Charlie; 'the sequel is to come. My visit to the monastery of Pierre Châtel had occurred in the month of

June. During the ensuing months I travelled over a considerable part of the south of France; and at length I crossed the Pyrenees, intending to proceed as far as Madrid, and winter there. Amongst the lions I had been recommended to visit was a monastery of Franciscans in the neighbourhood of Burgos, and I turned somewhat out of my road for the purpose of inspecting some curious manuscripts which the monks were reputed to possess. It was in the month of October, and a bright moonlight night, when I rang the bell, and requested to see the Padre Pachorra, to whom I had letters of introduction. I found him a dark, grave, sombre-looking man, not very unlike my old friend Brother Lazarus; and although he received me civilly enough, there was something in his demeanour that affected my spirits. The whole air of the convent, too, was melancholy; convents, like other establishments, taking their tone very much from the character of their superiors.

'As the monks had already supped when I arrived, I was served with some refreshment in the parlour; and the whole internal arrangements here being exceedingly strict, I immediately afterwards retired to my chamber, firmly resolved to take my departure the next day. I am not in the habit of going to bed early, and when I do, I never can sleep. By the time my usual sleeping hour is arrived, I have generally got so restless and nervous from lying awake, that slumber is banished altogether. Consequently, whenever I am under circumstances that oblige me to retire early to my room, I make a practice of reading till I find my eyelids heavy. But the dormitory assigned me in this Franciscan convent was so chilly, and the lamp gave so little light, that either remaining out of bed or reading in it was out of the question; so I yielded to necessity, and stretched myself on Padre Pachorra's hard couch; and a very hard one it was, I assure you. I was very cold too. There were not coverings enough on the bed to keep in my animal heat; and although I spread my own clothes over me also, still I lay shivering in a very uncomfortable manner, and, I am afraid, uttering sundry harsh remarks on the Padre's niggardly hospitality.

'In this agreeable occupation, as you may suppose, the flight of time was somewhat of the slowest. I do not know how many hours I had been there, but I had begun to think it never would be morning, when I heard something stirring in the gallery outside my door. The silence of a convent at night is the silence of the grave. Too far removed from the busy world without for external sounds to penetrate the thick walls, whilst within no slamming door, nor wandering foot, nor sacrilegious voice breaks in upon the stillness, the slightest noise strikes upon the ear with a fearful distinctness. I had no shutters to my window, so that I was aware it was still pitch-dark without, though, within, the feeble light of my lamp enabled me to see a little about me. I knew that the inmates of monasteries not only rise before daylight, but also that they perform midnight masses, and so forth; but then I had always observed that on these occasions they were summoned by a bell. Now, there was no bell; on the contrary, all was still as death, except the cautious foot which seemed to be approaching my room. "What on earth can it be?" thought I, sitting up in bed with an indescribable feeling of apprehension. At that moment a hand was laid upon the latch of my door. I cannot tell why, but instinctively I jumped out of bed – the door opened, and in walked what appeared to me to be Brother Lazarus, exactly as the Prior of Pierre Châtel had described him to me on the occasion of his nocturnal visit to his chamber. His eyes were open, but glazed, as of one dead; his face was of a ghastly paleness; he had nothing on but the grey tunic in which he slept; and in his hand he held a knife, such an one as was used by the monks to cut their large loaves with.

'You may conceive my amazement,' continued Charlie Lisle, whilst amongst his auditors every eye was firmly riveted. 'I rubbed my eyes, and asked myself if I were dreaming. Too surely I was awake – I had never even slumbered for an instant. Was I mad? I did not think I was; but certainly that was no proof to the contrary; and I almost began to doubt that Brother Lazarus was dead and buried on the other side of the Pyrenees. The Prior of Pierre Châtel had told me he was dead, and I had heard several others of the brotherhood alluding to his decease. I had seen his grave made ready, and I had passed his coffin as I descended to the hall; yet here he was in Spain, again rehearsing the frightful scene that Jolivet had described to me! Whilst all this was fleeting through my mind, I was standing *en chemise* betwixt the bed and the wall, on which side I had happened to leap out. In the meantime the apparition advanced with bare feet, and with the greatest caution, towards the other side of the bed; and as there were of course no curtains, I had a full view of his diabolical features, which appeared contracted with rage and malignity. As Jolivet had described to me, he first felt the bed, as if to ascertain if I were there; and I confess I was frightened out of my senses lest he should discover that I was not, and possibly detect me where I was. What could I have done, unarmed, and in my shirt, against this preternatural-looking monster? And to wake him – provided always it was really Brother Lazarus, and not his double, a point about which I felt exceedingly uncertain – I had learnt from Jolivet was extremely perilous. However, he did not discover that the bed was empty – his dream no doubt supplying a visionary victim for the occasion – and raising his arm, he plunged the knife into the mattress with a fierce determination that convinced me I should have had very little chance of surviving the blow had I been where he imagined me. Again and again he struck, I looking on with a horror that words could but feebly paint; and then he suddenly started, the uplifted arm was arrested – the pursuer was at hand: he first rushed to the window, and opened it, but being only a small lattice, there was no egress there, so he turned to the door, making his escape that way; and I could hear his foot distinctly flying along the gallery till he reached his own cell. By this time I was perfectly satisfied that it was no spirit I had seen, but the veritable Brother Lazarus, or Dominique, or whatever his name was – for he might have half a dozen *aliases* for aught I knew – though how he had contrived to come to life again, if he were dead, or by what means, or for what purpose, he could have persuaded the monks of Pierre Châtel of his decease, if the fact were not so, I could not conceive. There was no fastening to my door, and the first question that occurred to me was, whether this diabolical dream of his was ever repeated twice in one night. I had often heard that the magic number of *three* is apt to prevail on these occasions; and if so, he might come back again. I confess I was horridly afraid that he would. In the meantime I found myself shivering with cold, and was, perforce, obliged to creep into the bed, where indeed I was not much warmer. Sleep was of course out of the question. I lay listening anxiously, expecting either the stealthy foot of Brother Lazarus, or the glad sound of the matin bell, that would summon the monks from their cells, and wondering which I should hear first. Fortunately for my nerves it was the latter; and with alacrity I jumped out of bed, dressed myself, and descended to the chapel.

'When I reached it, the monks were on their knees, and their cowls being over their heads, I could not, as I ran my eye over them, distinguish my friend the somnambulist; but when they rose to their feet, his tall gaunt figure and high shoulders were easily discernible, and I had identified him before I saw his face. As they passed out of the chapel, I drew near and saluted him, observing that I believed I had had the pleasure of seeing him before at Pierre Châtel; but he only shook his head, as if in token of denial; and as I could obtain no other answer to my further attempts at conversation, I left him, and proceeded to pay my respects to the prior. Of course I felt it my duty to mention my adventure of the previous night, for Brother Lazarus might on some occasion chance to act out his dream more effectually than he had had the opportunity of doing with me and Père Jolivet.

' "I am extremely sorry indeed," said Padre Pachorra, when he had heard my story; "they must have omitted to lock him into his cell last night. I must speak about it, for the consequences might have been very serious."

' "Very serious to me certainly," said I. "But how is it I see this man here alive? When I quitted Pierre Châtel I was told he was dead, and I saw the preparations for his burial."

' "They believed him dead," returned the prior; "but he was only in a trance; and after he was screwed down in his coffin, just as they were about to lower it into the grave, they felt something was moving within. They opened it, and Fra Dominique was found alive. It appeared, from his own account, that he had been suffering extremely from his dreadful dream, on occasion of the visit of some young stranger – an Englishman, I think."

' "Myself, I have no doubt," said I.

' "Probably," returned the prior; "and this was either the cause, or the consequence of his illness, for it is difficult to decide which."

' "But how came he here?" I inquired.

' "It was in this monastery he commenced his vocation," answered the padre. "He was only at Pierre Châtel by indulgence, and after this accident they did not wish to retain him."

' "I do not wonder at that, I am sure," said I. "But why did he deny having been there? When I spoke of it to him just now, he only shook his head."

' "He did not mean to deny it, I daresay," said the prior; "but he never speaks. Fra Dominique has taken a vow of eternal silence." '

Here Charles Lisle brought his story to a conclusion. 'How extremely shocking!' exclaimed Lady Araminta; whilst the whole company agreed that he had made out an excellent excuse for wishing to sleep with his door locked, and that he had very satisfactorily entitled himself to the promised exchange.

The North Mail

by Amelia B. Edwards

Amelia Blandford Edwards (1831–1892) first showed her literary talent at the precocious age of seven when she had a poem published. Later she trained to be a musician but the sale of a story to Chamber's Journal *set her upon a writing career in which she proved remarkably prolific. In one fifteen year period she produced eight novels, three travel books, several volumes of poetry and historical research and many reviews, essays and stories contributed to popular magazines.*

In 1873 she visited Egypt, an experience which profoundly affected the course of her life. Thenceforth she gave herself over to the study of its ancient civilisations and their surviving monuments. Her work in this field not only led to priceless relics being rescued from destruction but led to a revival of interest in Egyptology in England and inspired several important expeditions. During a lecture tour of America in 1889, she fell and broke her arm. She never recovered her health and died three years later. Amelia Edwards wrote some fine stories of the supernatural, amongst them the classic A Night on the Borders of the Black Forest.

The following story, published in 1866, is no less excellent.

THE circumstances I am about to relate to you have truth to recommend them. They happened to myself, and my recollection of them is as vivid as if they had taken place only yesterday. Twenty years, however, have gone by since that night. During those twenty years I have told the story to but one other person. I tell it now with a reluctance which I find it difficult to overcome. All I entreat, meanwhile, is that you will abstain from forcing your own conclusions upon me. I want nothing explained away. I desire no arguments. My mind on this subject is quite made up; and, having the testimony of my own senses to rely upon, I prefer to abide by it.

Well! It was just twenty years ago, and within a day or two of the end of the grouse season. I had been out all day with my gun, and had had no sport to speak of. The wind was due east; the month, December; the place, a bleak wide moor in the far north of England. And I had lost my way. It was not a pleasant place in which to lose one's way, with the first feathery flakes of a coming snow-storm just fluttering down upon the heather, and the leaden evening closing in all around. I shaded my eyes with my hand, and stared anxiously into the gathering darkness, where the purple moorland melted into a range of low hills, some ten or twelve miles distant. Not the faintest smoke-wreath, not the tiniest cultivated patch, or fence, or sheep-track, met my eyes in any direction. There was nothing for it but to walk on, and take my chance of finding what shelter I could, by the way. So I shouldered my gun again, and pushed wearily forward; for I had been on foot since an hour after daybreak, and had eaten nothing since breakfast.

Meanwhile, the snow began to come down with ominous steadiness, and the wind fell. After this, the cold grew more intense, and the night came rapidly up. As for me, my prospects darkened with the darkening sky, and my heart grew heavy as I thought how my young wife was already watching for me through the window of our little inn parlour, and imagined all the suffering in store for her throughout this weary night. We had been married four months, and, having spent our autumn in the Highlands, were now lodging in a remote little village situated just on the verge of the great English moorlands. We were very much in love, and, of course, very happy. This morning, when we parted, she had implored me to return before dusk, and I had promised her that I would. What would I not have given to keep my word!

Even now, weary as I was, I felt that with a supper, an hour's rest, and a guide, I might still get back to her before midnight, if only guide and shelter could be found.

And all this time the snow fell, and the night thickened. I stopped and shouted every now and then, but my shouts seemed only to make the silence deeper. Then a vague sense of uneasiness came upon me, and I began to remember stories of travellers who had walked on and on in the falling snow until, wearied out, they were fain to lie down and sleep their lives away. Would it be possible, I asked myself, to keep on thus through all the long dark night? Would there not come a time when my limbs must fail, and my resolution give way? When I, too, must sleep the sleep of death. Death! I shuddered. How hard to die just now, when life lay all so bright before me! How hard for my darling, whose whole loving heart . . . but that thought was not to be borne! To banish it, I shouted again, louder and longer, and then listened eagerly. Was my shout answered, or did I only fancy that I heard a far-off cry? I halloed again, and again the echo followed. Then a wavering speck of light came suddenly out of the dark, shifting, disappearing, growing momentarily nearer and brighter. Running towards it at full speed, I found myself, to my great joy, face to face with an old man and a lantern.

'Thank God!' was the exclamation that burst involuntarily from my lips.

Blinking and frowning, he lifted the lantern and peered into my face.

'What for?' growled he, sulkily.

'Well – for you. I began to fear I should be lost in the snow.'

'Eh, then, folks do get cast away hereabouts fra' time to time, an' what's to hinder you from bein' cast away likewise, if the Lord's so minded?'

'If the Lord is so minded that you and I shall be lost together, friend, we must submit,' I replied; 'but I don't mean to be lost without you. How far am I now from Dwolding?'

'A gude twenty mile, more or less.'

'And the nearest village?'

'The nearest village is Wyke, an' that's twelve mile t'other side.'

'Where do you live, then?'

'Out yonder,' said he, with a vague jerk of the lantern.

'You're going home, I presume?'

'Maybe I am.'

'Then I'm going with you.'

The old man shook his head, and rubbed his nose reflectively with the handle of the lantern.

'It ain't o' no use,' growled he. 'He 'ont let you in – not he.'

'We'll see about that,' I replied, briskly. 'Who is He?'

'The master.'

'Who is the master?'

'That's now't to you,' was the unceremonious reply.

'Well, well; you lead the way, and I'll engage that the master shall give me shelter and a supper tonight.'

'Eh, you can try him!' muttered my reluctant guide; and, still shaking his head, he hobbled, gnome-like, away through the falling snow.

A large mass loomed up presently out of the darkness, and a huge dog rushed out barking furiously.

'Is this the house?' I asked.

'Ay, it's the house. Down, Bey!' And he fumbled in his pocket for the key.

I drew up close behind him, prepared to lose no chance of entrance, and saw in the little circle of light shed by the lantern that the door was heavily studded with iron nails, like the door of a prison. In another minute he had turned the key, and I had pushed past him into the house.

Once inside, I looked round with curiosity, and found myself in a great raftered hall, which served, apparently, a variety of uses. One end was piled to the roof with corn, like a barn. The other was stored with flour-sacks, agricultural implements, casks, and all kinds of miscellaneous lumber;

while from the beams overhead hung rows of hams, flitches, and bunches of dried herbs for winter use. In the centre of the floor stood some huge object gauntly dressed in a dingy wrapping-cloth, and reaching halfway to the rafters. Lifting a corner of this cloth, I saw, to my surprise, a telescope of very considerable size, mounted on a rude moveable platform with four small wheels. The tube was made of painted wood, bound round with bands of metal rudely fashioned; the speculum, so far as I could estimate its size by the dim light, measured at least fifteen inches in diameter. While I was yet examining the instrument, and asking myself whether it was not the work of some self-taught optician, a bell rang sharply.

'That's for you,' said my guide, with a malicious grin. 'Yonder's his room.'

He pointed to a low black door at the opposite side of the hall. I crossed over, rapped somewhat loudly, and went in, without waiting for an invitation. A huge, white-haired old man rose from a table covered with books and papers, and confronted me sternly.

'Who are you?' said he. 'How came you here? What do you want?'

'James Murray, barrister-at-law. On foot across the moor. Meat, drink, and sleep.'

He bent his bushy brows in a portentous frown.

'Mine is not a house of entertainment,' he said, haughtily. 'Jacob, how dared you admit this stranger?'

'I didn't admit him,' grumbled the old man. 'He followed me over the muir, and shouldered his way in before me. I'm no match for six foot two.'

'And pray, sir, by what right have you forced an entrance into my house?'

'The same by which I should have clung to your boat, if I were drowning. The right of self-preservation.'

'Self-preservation?'

'There's an inch of snow on the ground already,' I replied briefly; 'and it will be deep enough to cover my body before daybreak.'

He strode to the window, pulled aside a heavy black curtain, and looked out.

'It is true,' he said. 'You can stay, if you choose, till morning. Jacob, serve the supper.'

With this he waved me to a seat, resumed his own, and became at once absorbed in the studies at which I had disturbed him.

I placed my gun in a corner, drew a chair to the hearth, and examined my quarters at leisure. Smaller and less incongruous in its arrangements than the hall, this room contained, nevertheless, much to awaken my curiosity. The floor was carpetless. The whitewashed walls were in parts scrawled over with strange diagrams, and in others covered with shelves crowded with philosophical instruments, the uses of many of which were unknown to me. On one side of the fireplace stood a bookcase filled with dingy folios; on the other, a small organ, fantastically decorated with painted carvings of mediaeval saints and devils. Through the half-opened door of a cupboard at the further end of the room, I saw a long array of geological specimens, surgical preparations, crucibles, retorts, and jars of chemicals; while on the mantelshelf beside me, amid a number of small objects, stood a model of the solar system, a small galvanic battery, and a microscope. Every chair had its burden. Every corner was heaped high with books. The very floor was littered over with maps, casts, papers, tracings, and learned lumber of all conceivable kinds.

I stared about me with an amazement increased by every fresh object upon which my eyes chanced to rest. So strange a room I had never seen; yet seemed it stranger still to find such a room in a lone farmhouse, amid these wild and solitary moors! Over and over again, I looked from my host to his surroundings, and from his surroundings back to my host, asking myself who and what he could be? His head was singularly fine; but it was more the head of a poet than a philosopher. Broad in the temples, prominent over the eyes, and clothed with a rough profusion of perfectly white hair, it had all the ideality and much of the ruggedness that characterises the head of Louis von Beethoven. There were the same deep lines about the mouth, and the same stern furrows in the brow. There was the same concentration of expression. While I was yet observing him, the door opened, and Jacob brought in the supper. His master then closed his book, rose, and with more courtesy of manner than he had yet shown, invited me to the table.

A dish of ham and eggs, a loaf of brown bread, and a bottle of admirable sherry, were placed before me.

'I have but the homeliest farmhouse fare to offer you, sir,' said my entertainer. 'Your appetite, I trust, will make up for the deficiencies of our larder.'

I had already fallen upon the viands, and now protested, with the enthusiasm of a starving sportsman, that I had never eaten anything so delicious.

He bowed stiffly, and sat down to his own supper, which consisted, primitively, of a jug of milk and a basin of porridge. We ate in silence, and, when we had done, Jacob removed the tray. I then drew my chair back to the fireside. My host, somewhat to my surprise, did the same, and turning abruptly towards me said: –

'Sir, I have lived here in strict retirement for three-and-twenty years. During that time, I have not seen as many strange faces, and I have not read a single newspaper. You are the first stranger who has crossed my threshold for more than four years. Will you favour me with a few words of information respecting that outer world from which I have parted company so long?'

'Pray interrogate me,' I replied. 'I am heartily at your service.'

He bent his head in acknowledgement; leaned forward, with his elbows resting on his knees, and his chin supported in the palms of his hands; stared fixedly into the fire, and proceeded to question me.

His inquiries related chiefly to scientific matters, with the later progress of which, as applied to the practical purposes of life, he was almost wholly unacquainted. No student of science myself, I replied as well as my slight information permitted; but the task was far from easy, and I was much relieved when, passing from interrogation to discussion, he began pouring forth his own conclusions upon the facts which I had been attempting to place before him. He talked, and I listened spell-bound. He talked till I believe he almost forgot my presence, and only thought aloud. I had never heard anything like it then; I have never heard anything like it since. Familiar with all systems of all philosophies, subtle in analysis, bold in generalisation, he poured forth his thoughts in an uninterrupted stream, and, still leaning forward in the same moody attitude with his eyes fixed upon the fire, wandered from topic to topic, from speculation to speculation, like an inspired dreamer. From practical science to mental philosophy; from electricity in the wire to electricity in the nerve; from Watts to Mesmer, from Mesmer to Reichenbach, from Reichenbach to Swedenborg, Spinoza, Condillac, Descartes, Berkeley, Aristotle, Plato, and the Magi and Mystics of the East, were transitions which, however bewildering in their variety and scope, seemed easy and harmonious upon his lips as sequences in music. By-and-by – I forget now by what link of conjecture or illustration – he passed on to that field which lies beyond the boundary line of even conjectural philosophy, and reaches no man knows whither. He spoke of the soul and its aspirations; of the spirit and its powers; of second sight; of prophecy; of those phenomena which, under the names of ghosts, spectres, and supernatural appearances, have been denied by the sceptics and attested by the credulous, of all ages.

'The world,' he said, 'grows hourly more and more sceptical of all that lies beyond its own narrow radius; and our men of science foster the fatal tendency. They condemn as fable all that resists experiment. They reject as false all that cannot be brought to the test of the laboratory or the dissecting-room. Against what superstition have they waged so long and obstinate a war, as against the belief in apparitions? And yet what superstition has maintained its hold upon the minds of men so long and so firmly? Show me any fact in physics, in history, in archaeology, which is supported by testimony so wide and so various. Attested by all races of men, in all ages, and in all climates, by the soberest sages of antiquity, by the rudest savages of today, by the Christian, the Pagan, the Pantheist, the Materialist, this phenomenon is treated as a nursery tale by the philosophers of our century. Circumstantial evidence weighs with them as a feather in the balance. The comparison of causes with effects, however valuable in physical science, is put aside as worthless and unreliable. The evidence of competent witnesses, however conclusive in a court of justice, counts for nothing. He who pauses before he pronounces, is condemned as a trifler. He who believes, is a dreamer or a fool.'

He spoke with bitterness, and, having said thus, relapsed for some minutes into silence. Presently he raised his head from his hands, and added, with an altered voice and manner –

'I, sir, paused, investigated, believed, and was not ashamed to state my convictions to the world. I, too, was branded as a visionary, held up to ridicule by my contemporaries, and hooted from that field of science in which I had laboured with honour during all the best years of my life. These things happened just three-and-twenty years ago. Since then, I have lived as you see me living now, and the world has forgotten me, as I have forgotten the world. You have my history.'

'It is a very sad one,' I murmured, scarcely knowing what to answer.

'It is a very common one,' he replied. 'I have only suffered for the truth, as many a better and wiser man has suffered before me.'

He rose, as if desirous of ending the conversation, and went over to the window.

'It has ceased snowing,' he observed, as he dropped the curtain, and came back to the fireside.

'Ceased!' I exclaimed, starting eagerly to my feet. 'Oh, if it were only possible – but no! it is hopeless. Even if I could find my way across the moor, I could not walk twenty miles tonight.'

'Walk twenty miles tonight!' repeated my host. 'What are you thinking of?'

'Of my wife,' I replied, impatiently. 'Of my young wife, who does not know that I have lost my way, and who is at this moment breaking her heart with suspense and terror.'

'Where is she?'

'At Dwolding, twenty miles away.'

'At Dwolding,' he echoed, thoughtfully. 'Yes, the distance, it is true, is twenty miles; but – are you so anxious to save the next six or eight hours?'

'So anxious, that I would give ten guineas at this moment for a guide and a horse.'

'Your wish can be gratified at a less costly rate,' said he, smiling. 'The night mail from the north, which changes horses at Dwolding, passes within five miles of this spot, and will be due at a certain cross-road in about an hour and a quarter. If Jacob were to go with you across the moor, and put you into the old coach road, you could find your way, I suppose, to where it joins the new one?'

'Easily – gladly.'

He smiled again, rang the bell, gave the old servant his directions, and, taking a bottle of whiskey and a wine-glass from the cupboard in which he kept his chemicals, said –

'The snow lies deep, and it will be difficult walking tonight on the moor. A glass of usquebaugh before you start.'

I would have declined the spirit, but he pressed it on me, and I drank it. It went down my throat like liquid flame, and almost took my breath away.

'It is strong,' he said; 'but it will help to keep out the cold. And now you have no moments to spare. Good night!'

I thanked him for his hospitality, and would have shaken hands, but that he had turned away before I could finish my sentence. In another minute I had traversed the hall, Jacob had locked the outer door behind me, and we were out on the wide white moor.

Although the wind had fallen, it was still bitterly cold. Not a star glimmered in the black vault overhead. Not a sound, save the rapid crunching of the snow beneath our feet, disturbed the heavy stillness of the night. Jacob, not too well pleased with his mission, shambled on before in sullen silence, his lantern in his hand, and his shadow at his feet. I followed, with my gun over my shoulder, as little inclined for conversation as himself. My thoughts were full of my late host. His voice yet rang in my ears. His eloquence yet held my imagination captive. I remember to this day, with surprise, how my over-excited brain retained whole sentences and parts of sentences, troops of brilliant images, and fragments of splendid reasoning, in the very words in which he had uttered them. Musing thus over what I had heard, and striving to recall a lost link here and there, I strode on at the heels of my guide, absorbed and unobservant. Presently – at the end, as it seemed to me, of only a few minutes – he came to a sudden halt, and said:

'Yon's your road. Keep the stone fence to your right hand, and you can't fail of the way.'

'This, then, is the old coach-road?'

'Ay, 'tis the old coach-road.'

'And how far do I go, before I reach the cross-roads?'

'Nigh upon three miles.'

I pulled out my purse, and he became more communicative.

'The road's a fair road enough,' said he, 'for foot passengers; but 'twas over steep and narrow for the northern traffic. You'll mind where the parapet's broken away, close again the sign-post. It's never been mended since the accident.'

'What accident?'

'Eh, the night mail pitched right over into the valley below – a gude sixty feet an' more – just at the worst bit o' road in the whole county.'

'Horrible! Were many lives lost?'

'All. Four were found dead, and t'other two died next morning.'

'How long is it since this happened?'

'Just nine year.'

'Near the sign-post, you say? I will bear it in mind. Good night.'

'Gude night, sir, and thankee.'

Jacob pocketed his half-crown, made a faint pretence of touching his hat, and trudged back by the way he had come.

I watched the light of his lantern till it quite disappeared, and then turned to pursue my way alone. This was no longer a matter of the slightest difficulty, for, despite the dead darkness overhead, the line of stone fence showed distinctly enough against the pale gleam of the snow. How silent it seemed now, with only my own footsteps to listen to; how silent and how solitary! A strange disagreeable sense of loneliness stole over me. I walked faster. I hummed a fragment of a tune. I cast up enormous sums in my head, and accumulated them at compound interest. I did my best, in short, to forget the startling speculations to which I had but just been listening and to some extent, I succeeded.

Meanwhile the night air seemed to become colder and colder, and though I walked fast, I found it impossible to keep myself warm. My feet were like ice. I lost sensation in my hands, and grasped my gun mechanically. I even breathed with difficulty, as though, instead of traversing a quiet north country highway, I were sealing the uppermost heights of some gigantic Alp. This last symptom became presently so distressing, that I was forced to stop for a few minutes, and lean against the stone fence. As I did so, I chanced to look back up the road, and there, to my infinite relief, I saw a distant point of light, like the gleam of an approaching lantern. I at first concluded that Jacob had retraced his steps and followed me; but even as the conjecture presented itself, a second light flashed into sight – a light evidently parallel with the first, and approaching at the same rate of motion. It needed no second thought to show me that these must be the carriage-lamps of some private vehicle; though it seemed strange that any private vehicle should take a road professedly disused and dangerous.

There could be no doubt, however, of the fact, for the lamps grew larger and brighter every moment, and I even fancied I could already see the dark outline of the carriage between them. It was coming up very fast, and quite noiselessly; the snow being nearly a foot deep under the wheels.

And now the body of the vehicle became distinctly visible behind the lamps. It looked strangely lofty. A sudden suspicion flashed upon me. Was it possible that I had passed the cross roads in the dark without observing the sign-post, and could this be the very coach which I had come to meet?

No need to ask myself that question a second time, for here it came round the bend of the road, guard and driver, one outside passenger, and four steaming greys, all wrapped in a soft haze of light, through which the lamps blazed out like a pair of fiery meteors.

I jumped forward, waved my hat, and shouted. The mail came down at full speed, and passed me. For a moment I feared that I had not been seen or heard, but it was only for a moment. The coachman pulled up; the guard, muffled to the eyes in capes and comforters, and apparently sound asleep in the rumble, neither answered my hail nor made the slightest effort to dismount; the outside passenger did not even turn his head. I opened the door for myself, and looked in. There were but three travellers inside, so I stepped in, shut the door, slipped into the vacant corner, and congratulated myself on my good fortune.

The atmosphere of the coach seemed, if possible, colder than that of the outer air, and was pervaded by a singularly damp and disagreeable smell. I looked round at my fellow passengers. They were all three men; and all silent. They did not seem to be asleep, but each leaned back in his corner of the vehicle, as if absorbed in his own reflections. I attempted to open a conversation.

'How intensely cold it is tonight,' I said, addressing my opposite neighbour.

He lifted his head, looked at me, but made no reply.

'The winter,' I added, 'seems to have begun in earnest.'

Although the corner in which he sat was so dim that I could distinguish none of his features very clearly, I saw that his eyes were still turned full upon me. And yet he answered never a word.

At any other time I should have felt, and perhaps expressed, some annoyance; but at that moment I felt too ill to do either. The icy coldness of the night air had struck a chill to my very marrow, and the strange smell inside the coach was affecting me with an intolerable nausea. I shivered from head to foot, and, turning to my left-hand neighbour, asked if he had any objection to an open window.

He neither spoke nor stirred.

I repeated the question somewhat more loudly, but with the same result. Then I lost patience, and let the sash down. As I did so, the leather strap broke in my hand, and I observed that the glass was covered with a thick coat of mildew, the accumulation, apparently, of years. My attention being thus drawn to the condition of the coach, I examined it more narrowly, and saw by the uncertain light of the outer lamps that it was in the last state of dilapidation. Every part of it was not only out of repair, but in a state of actual decay. The sashes splintered at a touch. The leather fittings were crusted over with mould, and literally rotting from the woodwork. The floor was almost breaking away beneath my feet. The whole machine, in short, was foul with damp, and had evidently been dragged from some outhouse in which it had been mouldering away for years, to do another day or two of duty on the road.

I turned to the third passenger, whom I had not yet addressed, and hazarded one more remark.

'This coach,' I said, 'is in a deplorable condition. The regular mail, I suppose, is under repair?'

He moved his head slowly, and looked me in the face, without speaking a word. I shall never forget that look while I live. I turned cold at heart under it. I turn cold at heart even now when I recall it. His eyes glowed with a fiery unnatural lustre. His face was livid as the face of a corpse. His bloodless lips were drawn back as if in the agony of death, and showed the gleaming teeth between.

The words that I was about to utter died upon my lips,

and a strange horror came upon me. My sight had by this time become used to the gloom of the coach, and I could see with tolerable distinctness. I turned to my opposite neighbour. He, too, was looking at me, with the same startling pallor in his face, and the same stony glitter in his eyes. I passed my hand across my brow. I turned to the passenger on the seat beside my own, and saw – oh Heaven! how shall I describe what I saw? I saw that he was no living man – that none of them were living men, like myself! A pale phosphorescent light – the light of putrefaction – played upon their awful faces; upon their hair, dank with the dews of the grave; upon their clothes, earth-stained and dropping to pieces; upon their hands, which were as the hands of corpses long buried. Only their eyes, their terrible eyes, were living; and those eyes were all turned menacingly upon me!

A shriek of terror, a wild unintelligible cry for help and mercy, burst from my lips as I flung myself against the door, and strove in vain to open it.

In that single instant, brief and vivid as a landscape beheld in the flash of summer lightning, I saw the moon shining down through a rift of stormy cloud – the ghastly sign-post rearing its warning finger by the wayside – the broken parapet – the plunging horses – the black gulf below. Then the coach reeled like a ship at sea. Then came a mighty crash – a sense of crushing pain – and then, darkness.

It seemed as if years had gone by, when I awoke one morning from a deep sleep, and found my wife watching by my bedside. I will pass over the scene that ensued, and give you, in half a dozen words, the tale she told me with tears of thanksgiving. I had fallen over a precipice, close against the junction of the old coach-road and the new, and had only been saved from certain death by lighting upon a deep snowdrift that had accumulated at the foot of the rock beneath. In this snowdrift I was discovered at daybreak by a couple of shepherds, who carried me to the nearest shelter, and brought a surgeon to my aid. The surgeon found me in a state of raving delirium, with a broken arm and a compound fracture of the skull. The letters in my pocket-book showed my name and address; my wife was summoned to nurse me; and, thanks to youth and a fine constitution, I came out of danger at last. The place of my fall, I need scarcely say, was precisely that at which a frightful accident had happened to the north mail nine years before.

I never told my wife the fearful events which I have just related to you. I told the surgeon who attended me; but he treated the whole adventure as a mere dream born of the fever in my brain. We discussed the question over and over again, until we found that we could discuss it with temper no longer, and then we dropped it. Others may form what conclusions they please – I *know* that twenty years ago I was the fourth inside passenger in that Phantom Coach.

The Old Nurse's Story

by Elizabeth Gaskell

Elizabeth Cleghorn Gaskell (1810–1865) was a leading figure amongst Victorian female writers. Her husband, William Gaskell, a clergyman, encouraged her early efforts but it was not until the death, from smallpox, of a small son in 1848 that she seriously undertook a writing career in order to escape her grief. Mary Barton, her first novel, was published in 1848 and its success drew her into the literary circles where she became a friend of Dickens, Carlyle, Wordsworth and other notables. More novels followed including Cranford, *and* Ruth *but Mrs Gaskell was chiefly a short story specialist. One of her best friends was Charlotte Brontë and in 1857 she published a valuable biography of the authoress of* Jane Eyre.

No anthology of this period would be complete without a good old Christmassy ghost story set in a brooding snow-bound mansion. And this is one of the best of them.

You know, my dears, that your mother was an orphan, and an only child; and I dare say you have heard that your grandfather was a clergyman up in Westmorland, where I come from. I was just a girl in the village school, when, one day, your grandmother came in to ask the mistress if there was any scholar there who would do for a nurse-maid; and mighty proud I was, I can tell ye, when the mistress called me up, and spoke to my being a good girl at my needle, and a steady honest girl, and one whose parents were very respectable, though they might be poor. I thought I should like nothing better than to serve the pretty young lady, who was blushing as deep as I was, as she spoke of the coming baby, and what I should have to do with it. However, I see you don't care so much for this part of my story, as for what you think is to come, so I'll tell you at once. I was engaged and settled at the parsonage before Miss Rosamond (that was the baby, who is now your mother) was born. To be sure, I had little enough to do with her when she came, for she was never out of her mother's arms, and slept by her all night long; and proud enough was I sometimes when missis trusted her to me. There never was such a baby before or since, though you've all of you been fine enough in your turns; but for sweet, winning ways, you've none of you come up to your mother. She took after her mother, who was a real lady born; a Miss Furnivall, a grand-daughter of Lord Furnivall's, in Northumberland. I believe she had neither brother nor sister, and had been brought up in my lord's family till she had married your grandfather, who was just a curate, son to a shopkeeper in Carlisle – but a clever, fine gentleman as ever was – and one who was a right-down hard worker in his parish, which was very wide, and scattered all abroad over the Westmorland Fells. When your mother, little Miss Rosamond, was about four or five years old, both her parents died in a fortnight – one after the other. Ah! that was a sad time. My pretty young mistress and me was looking for another baby, when my master came home from one of his long rides, wet, and tired, and took the fever he died of; and then she never held up her head again, but just lived to see her dead baby, and have it laid on her breast before she sighed away her life. My mistress had asked me, on her death-bed, never to leave Miss Rosamond; but if she had never spoken a word, I would have gone with the little child to the end of the world.

The next thing, and before we had well stilled our sobs, the executors and guardians came to settle the affairs. They were my poor young mistress's own cousin, Lord Furnivall, and Mr Esthwaite, my master's brother, a shopkeeper in Manchester; not so well to do then, as he was afterwards, and with a large family rising about him. Well! I don't know if it were their settling, or because of a letter my mistress wrote on her death-bed to her cousin, my lord; but somehow it was settled that Miss Rosamond and me were to go to Furnivall Manor House, in Northumberland, and my lord spoke as if it had been her mother's wish that she should live with his family, and as if he had no objections, for that one or two more or less could make no difference in so grand a household. So, though that was not the way in which I should have wished the coming of my bright and pretty pet to have been looked at – who was like a sunbeam in any family, be it never so grand – I was well pleased that all the folks in the Dale should stare and admire, when they heard I was going to be young lady's maid at my Lord Furnivall's at Furnivall Manor.

But I made a mistake in thinking we were to go and live where my lord did. It turned out that the family had left Furnivall Manor House fifty years or more. I could not hear that my poor young mistress had ever been there, though she had been brought up in the family; and I was sorry for that, for I should have liked Miss Rosamond's youth to have passed where her mother's had been.

My lord's gentleman, from whom I asked as many questions as I durst, said that the Manor House was at the foot of the Cumberland Fells, and a very grand place; that an old Miss Furnivall, a great-aunt of my lord's, lived there, with only a few servants; but that it was a very healthy place, and my lord had thought that it would suit Miss Rosamond very well for a few years, and that her being there might perhaps amuse his old aunt.

I was bidden by my lord to have Miss Rosamond's things ready by a certain day. He was a stern proud man, as they say all the Lords Furnivall were; and he never spoke a word more than was necessary. Folk did say he had loved my young mistress; but that, because she knew that his father would object, she would never listen to him, and married Mr Esthwaite; but I don't know. He never married at any rate. But he never took much notice of Miss Rosamond; which I thought he might have done if he had cared for her dead mother. He sent his gentleman with us to the Manor House, telling him to join him at Newcastle that same evening; so there was no great length of time for him to make us known to all the strangers before he, too, shook us off; and we were left, two lonely young things (I was not eighteen), in the great old Manor House. It seems like yesterday that we drove there. We had left our own dear parsonage very early, and we had both cried as if our hearts would break, though we were travelling in my lord's carriage, which I thought so much of once. And now it was long past noon on a September day, and we stopped to change horses for the last time at a little smoky town, all full of colliers and miners. Miss Rosamond had fallen asleep, but Mr Henry told me to waken her, that she might see the park and the Manor House as we drove up. I thought it rather a pity; but I did what he bade me, for fear he should complain of me to my lord. We had left all signs of a town, or even a village, and were then inside the gates of a large wild park – not like the parks here in the south, but with rocks, and the noise of running water, and gnarled thorn-trees, and old oaks, all white and peeled with age.

The road went up about two miles, and then we saw a great and stately house, with many trees close around it, so close that in some places their branches dragged against the walls when the wind blew; and some hung broken down; for no one seemed to take much charge of the place; – to lop the wood, or to keep the moss-covered carriage-way in order. Only in front of the house all was clear. The great oval drive was without a weed; and neither tree nor creeper was allowed to grow over the long, many-windowed front; at both sides of which a wing projected, which were each the ends of other side fronts; for the house, although it was so desolate, was even grander than I expected. Behind it rose the Fells, which seemed unenclosed and bare enough; and on the left hand of the house, as you stood facing it, was a little, old-fashioned flower-garden, as I found out afterwards. A door opened out upon it from the west front; it had been scooped out of the thick dark wood for some old Lady Furnivall; but the branches of the great forest trees had grown and overshadowed it again, and there were very few flowers that would live there at that time.

When we drove up to the great front entrance, and went into the hall I thought we should be lost – it was so large, and vast, and grand. There was a chandelier all of bronze, hung down from the middle of the ceiling; and I had never seen one before, and looked at it all in amaze. Then, at one end of the hall, was a great fire-place, as large as the sides of the houses in my country, with massy andirons and dogs to hold the wood; and by it were heavy old-fashioned sofas. At the opposite end of the hall, to the left as you went in – on the western side – was an organ built into the wall, and so large that it filled up the best part of that end. Beyond it, on the same side, was a door; and opposite, on each side of the fire-place, were also doors leading to the east front; but those I never went through as long as I stayed in the house, so I can't tell you what lay beyond.

The afternoon was closing in and the hall, which had no fire lighted in it, looked dark and gloomy, but we did not stay there a moment. The old servant, who had opened the door for us bowed to Mr Henry, and took us in through the door at the further side of the great organ, and led us through several smaller halls and passages into the west drawing-room, where he said that Miss Furnivall was sitting. Poor little Miss Rosamond held very tight to me, as if she were scared and lost in that great place, and as for myself, I was not much better. The west drawing-room was very cheerful-looking, with a warm fire in it, and plenty of good, comfortable furniture about. Miss Furnivall was an old lady not far from eighty, I should think, but I do not know. She was thin and tall, and had a face as full of fine wrinkles as if they had been drawn all over it with a needle's point. Her eyes were very watchful to make up, I suppose, for her being so deaf as to be obliged to use a trumpet. Sitting with her, working at the same great piece of tapestry, was Mrs Stark, her maid and companion, and almost as old as she was. She had lived with Miss Furnivall ever since they both were young, and now she seemed more like a friend than a servant; she looked so cold and grey, and stony, as if she had never loved or cared for any one; and I don't suppose she did care for any one, except her mistress; and, owing to the great deafness of the latter, Mrs Stark treated her very much as if she were a child. Mr Henry gave some message from my lord, and then he bowed good-bye to us all, – taking no notice of my sweet little Miss Rosamond's out-stretched hand – and left us standing there, being looked at by the two old ladies through their spectacles.

I was right glad when they rung for the old footman who had shown us in at first, and told him to take us to our rooms. So we went out of that great drawing-room, and into another sitting-room, and out of that, and then up a great flight of stairs, and along a broad gallery — which was something like a library, having books all down one side, and windows and writing-tables all down the other – till we came to our rooms, which I was not sorry to hear were just over the kitchens; for I began to think I should be lost in that wilderness of a house. There was an old nursery, that had been used for all the little lords and ladies long ago, with a pleasant fire burning in the grate, and the kettle boiling on the hob, and tea things spread out on the table; and out of that room was the night-nursery, with a little crib for Miss Rosamond close to my bed. And old James called up Dorothy, his wife, to bid us welcome; and both he and she were so hospitable and kind, that by and by Miss Rosamond and me felt quite at home; and by the time tea was over, she was sitting on Dorothy's knee, and chattering away as fast as her little tongue could go. I soon found out that Dorothy was from Westmorland, and that bound her and me together, as it were; and I would never wish to meet with kinder people than were old James and his wife. James had lived pretty nearly all his life in my lord's family, and thought there was no one so grand as they. He even looked down a little on his wife; because, till he had married her, she had never lived in any but a farmer's household. But he was very fond of her, as well he might be. They had one servant under them, to do all the rough work. Agnes they called her; and she and me, and James and Dorothy, with Miss Furnivall and Mrs Stark, made up the family; always remembering my sweet little Miss Rosamond. I used to wonder what they had done before she came, they thought so much of her now. Kitchen and drawing-room, it was all the same. The hard, sad Miss Furnivall, and the cold Mrs Stark, looked pleased when she came fluttering in like a bird, playing and pranking hither and thither, with a continual murmur, and pretty prattle of gladness. I am sure, they were sorry many a time when she flitted away into the kitchen, though they were too proud to ask her to stay with them, and were a little surprised at her taste; though to be sure, as Mrs Stark said, it was not to be wondered at, remembering what stock her father had come of. The great, old rambling house, was a famous place for little Miss Rosamond. She made expeditions all over it, with me at her heels; all, except the east wing, which was never opened, and whither we never thought of going. But in the western and northern part was many a pleasant room; full of things that were curiosities to us, though they might not have been to people who had seen more. The windows were darkened by the sweeping boughs of the trees, and the ivy which had overgrown them: but, in the green gloom, we could manage to see old China jars and carved ivory boxes, and great heavy books, and, above all, the old pictures!

Once, I remember, my darling would have Dorothy go with us to tell us who they all were; for they were all portraits of some of my lord's family, though Dorothy could not tell us the names of every one. We had gone through most of the rooms, when we came to the old state drawing-room over the hall, and there was a picture of Miss Furnivall; or, as she was called in those days, Miss Grace, for she was the younger sister. Such a beauty she must have been! but with such a set, proud look, and such scorn looking out of her handsome eyes, with her eyebrows just a little raised, as if she wondered how any one could have the impertinence to look at her; and her lip curled at us, as we stood there gazing. She had a dress on, the like of which I had never seen before, but it was all the fashion when she was young: a hat of some soft white stuff like beaver, pulled a little over her brows, and a beautiful plume of feathers sweeping round it on one side; and her gown of blue satin was open in front to a quilted white stomacher.

'Well, to be sure!' said I, when I had gazed my fill. 'Flesh is grass, they do say; but who would have thought that Miss Furnivall had been such an out-and-out beauty, to see her now?'

'Yes,' said Dorothy. 'Folks change sadly. But if what my master's father used to say was true, Miss Furnivall, the elder sister, was handsomer than Miss Grace. Her picture is here somewhere; but, if I show it you, you must never let on, even to James, that you have seen it. Can the little lady hold her tongue, think you?' asked she.

I was not so sure, for she was such a little sweet, bold, open-spoken child, so I set her to hide herself; and then I helped Dorothy to turn a great picture, that leaned with its face towards the wall, and was not hung up as the others were. To be sure, it beat Miss Grace for beauty; and, I think, for scornful pride, too, though in that matter it might be hard to choose. I could have looked at it an hour, but Dorothy seemed half frightened at having shown it to me, and hurried it back again, and bade me run and find Miss Rosamond, for that there were some ugly places about the house, where she should like ill for the child to go. I was a brave, high-spirited girl, and thought little of what the old woman said, for I liked hide-and-seek as well as any child in the parish; so off I ran to find my little one.

As winter drew on, and the days grew shorter, I was sometimes almost certain that I heard a noise as if some one was playing on the great organ in the hall. I did not hear it every evening; but, certainly, I did very often; usually when I was sitting with Miss Rosamond, after I had put her to bed, and keeping quite still and silent in the bedroom. Then I used to hear it booming and swelling away in the distance. The first night, when I went down to my supper, I asked Dorothy who had been playing music, and James said very shortly that I was a gowk to take the wind soughing among the trees for music; but I saw Dorothy look at him very fearfully, and Bessy, the kitchen-maid, said something beneath her breath, and went quite white. I saw they did not like my question, so I held my peace till I was with Dorothy alone, when I knew I could get a good deal out of her. So, the next day, I watched my time, and I coaxed and asked her who it was that played the organ; for I knew that it was the organ and not the wind well enough, for all I had kept silence before James. But Dorothy had had her lesson I'll warrant, and never a word could I get from her. So then I tried Bessy, though I had always held my head rather above her, as I was evened to James and Dorothy, and she was little better than their servant. So she said I must never, never tell; and if I ever told, I was never to say *she* had told me; but it was a very strange noise, and she had heard it many a time, but most of all on winter nights, and before storms; and folks did say, it was the old lord playing on the great organ in the hall, just as he used to do when he was alive; but who the old lord was, or why he played, and why he played on stormy winter evenings in particular, she either could not or would not tell me. Well! I told you I had a brave heart; and I thought it was rather pleasant to have that grand music rolling about the house, let who would be the player; for now it rose above the great gusts of wind, and wailed and triumphed just like a living creature, and then it fell to a softness most complete; only it was always music, and tunes, so it was nonsense to call it the wind. I thought at first, that it might be Miss Furnivall who played, unknown to Bessy; but, one day when I was in the hall by myself, I opened the organ and peeped all about it and around it, as I had done to the organ in Crosthwaite Church once before, and I saw it was all broken and destroyed inside, though it looked so brave and fine; and then, though it was noon-day, my flesh began to creep a little, and I shut it up, and run away pretty quickly to my own bright nursery; and I did not like hearing the music for some time after that, any more than James and Dorothy did. All this time Miss Rosamond was making herself more, and more beloved. The old ladies liked her to dine with them at their early dinner; James stood behind Miss Furnivall's chair, and I behind Miss Rosamond's all in state; and, after dinner, she would play about in a corner of the great drawing-room, as still as any mouse, while Miss Furnivall slept, and I had my dinner in the kitchen. But she was glad enough to come to me in the nursery afterwards; for, as she said, Miss Furnivall was so sad, and Mrs Stark so dull; but she and I were merry enough; and, by-and-by, I got not to care for that weird rolling music, which did one no harm, if we did not know where it came from.

That winter was very cold. In the middle of October the frosts began, and lasted many, many weeks. I remember, one day at dinner, Miss Furnivall lifted up her sad, heavy eyes, and said to Mrs Stark, 'I am afraid we shall have a terrible winter,' in a strange kind of meaning way. But Mrs Stark pretended not to hear, and talked very loud of something else. My little lady and I did not care for the frost; not we! As long as it was dry we climbed up the steep brows, behind the house, and went up on the Fells, which were bleak, and bare enough, and there we ran races in the fresh, sharp air; and once we came down by a new path that took us past the two old gnarled holly-trees, which grew about half-way down by the east side of the house. But the days grew shorter, and shorter; and the old lord, if it was he, played away more, and more stormily and sadly on the great organ. One Sunday afternoon, – it must have been towards the end of November – I asked Dorothy to take charge of little Missey when she came out of the drawing-room, after Miss Furnivall had had her nap; for it was too cold to take her with me to church, and yet I wanted to go. And Dorothy was glad enough to promise, and was so fond of the child that all seemed well; and Bessy and I set off very briskly, though the sky hung heavy and black over the white earth, as if the night had never fully gone away; and the air, though still, was very biting and keen.

'We shall have a fall of snow,' said Bessy to me. And sure enough, even while we were in church, it came down thick, in great large flakes, so thick it almost darkened the windows. It had stopped snowing before we came out, but it lay soft, thick and deep beneath our feet, as we tramped home. Before we got to the hall the moon rose, and I think it was lighter then, – what with the moon, and what with the white dazzling snow – than it had been when we went to church, between two and three o'clock. I have not told you that Miss Furnivall and Mrs Stark never went to church: they used to read the prayers together, in their quiet gloomy way; they seemed to feel the Sunday very long without their tapestry-work to be busy at. So when I went to Dorothy in the kitchen, to fetch Miss Rosamond and take her upstairs with me, I did not much wonder when the old woman told me that the ladies had kept the child with them, and that she had never come to the kitchen, as I had bidden her, when she was tired of behaving pretty in the drawing-room. So I took off my things and went to find her, and bring her to her supper in the nursery. But when I went into the best drawing-room, there sat the two old ladies, very still and quiet, dropping out a word now and then, but looking as if nothing so bright and merry as Miss Rosamond had ever been near them. Still I thought she might be hiding from me; it was one of her pretty ways; and that she had persuaded them to look as if they knew nothing about her; so I went softly peeping under this sofa, and behind that chair, making believe I was sadly frightened at not finding her.

'What's the matter, Hester?' said Mrs Stark sharply. I don't know if Miss Furnivall had seen me, for, as I told you, she was very deaf, and she sat quite still, idly staring into the fire, with her hopeless face. 'I'm only looking for my little Rosy-Posy,' replied I, still thinking that the child was there, and near me, though I could not see her.

'Miss Rosamond is not here,' said Mrs Stark. 'She went

away more than an hour ago to find Dorothy.' And she too turned and went on looking into the fire.

My heart sank at this, and I began to wish I had never left my darling. I went back to Dorothy and told her. James was gone out for the day, but she and me and Bessy took lights and went up into the nursery first, and then we roamed over the great large house, calling and entreating Miss Rosamond to come out of her hiding place, and not frighten us to death in that way. But there was no answer; no sound.

'Oh!' said I at last, 'Can she have got into the east wing and hidden there?'

But Dorothy said it was not possible, for that she herself had never been in there; that the doors were always locked, and my lord's steward had the keys, she believed; at any rate, neither she, nor James had ever seen them: so, I said I would go back, and see if, after all, she was not hidden in the drawing-room, unknown to the old ladies; and if I found her there, I said, I would whip her well for the fright she had given me; but I never meant to do it. Well, I went back to the west drawing-room, and I told Mrs Stark we could not find her anywhere, and asked for leave to look all about the furniture there, for I thought now, that she might have fallen asleep in some warm hidden corner; but no! we looked, Miss Furnivall got up and looked, trembling all over, and she was nowhere there; then we set off again, every one in the house, and looked in all the places we had searched before, but we could not find her. Miss Furnivall shivered and shook so much, that Mrs Stark took her back into the warm drawing-room; but not before they had made me promise to bring her to them when she was found. Well-a-day! I began to think she never would be found, when I bethought me to look out into the great front court, all covered with snow. I was upstairs when I looked out; but, it was such clear moonlight, I could see quite plain two little footprints, which might be traced from the hall door, and round the corner of the east wing. I don't know how I got down, but I tugged open the great, stiff hall door; and, throwing the skirt of my gown over my head for a cloak, I ran out. I turned the east corner, and there a black shadow fell on the snow; but when I came again into the moonlight, there were the little footmarks going up – up to the Fells. It was bitter cold; so cold that the air almost took the skin off my face as I ran, but I ran on, crying to think how my poor little darling must be perished, and frightened. I was within sight of the holly-trees, when I saw a shepherd coming down the hill, bearing something in his arms wrapped in his maud. He shouted to me, and asked me if I had lost a bairn; and, when I could not speak for crying, he bore towards me, and I saw my wee bairnie lying still, and white, and stiff, in his arms, as if she had been dead. He told me he had been up the Fells to gather in his sheep, before the deep cold of night came on, and that under the holly-trees (black marks on the hill-side, where no other bush was for miles around) he had found my little lady – my lamb – my queen – my darling – stiff, and cold, in the terrible sleep which is frost-begotten. Oh! the joy, and the tears of having her in my arms once again! for I would not let him carry her; but took her, maud and all, into my own arms, and held her near my own warm neck, and heart, and felt the life stealing slowly back again into her little gentle limbs. But she was still insensible when we reached the hall, and I had no breath for speech. We went in by the kitchen door.

'Bring the warming-pan,' said I; and I carried her upstairs and began undressing her by the nursery fire, which Bessy had kept up. I called my little lammie all the sweet and playful names I could think of, – even while my eyes were blinded by my tears; and at last, oh! at length she opened her large blue eyes. Then I put her into her warm bed, and sent Dorothy down to tell Miss Furnivall that all was well; and I made up my mind to sit by my darling's bedside the live-long night. She fell away into a soft sleep as soon as her pretty head had touched the pillow, and I watched by her till morning light; when she wakened up bright and clear – or so I thought at first – and, my dears, so I think now.

She said, that she had fancied that she should like to go to Dorothy, for that both the old ladies were asleep, and it was very dull in the drawing-room; and that, as she was going through the west lobby, she saw the snow through the high window falling – falling – soft and steady; but she wanted to see it lying pretty and white on the ground; so she made her way into the great hall; and then, going to the window, she saw it bright and soft upon the drive; but while she stood there, she saw a little girl, not so old as she was, 'but so pretty,' said my darling, 'and this little girl beckoned to me to come out; and oh, she was so pretty and so sweet I could not choose but go.' And then this other little girl had taken her by the hand, and side by side the two had gone round the east corner.

'Now you are a naughty little girl, and telling stories,' said I. 'What would your good mamma, that is in heaven, and never told a story in her life, say to her little Rosamond, if she heard her – and I dare say she does – telling stories!'

'Indeed, Hester,' sobbed out my child, 'I'm telling you true. Indeed I am.'

'Don't tell me!' said I, very stern. 'I tracked you by your foot-marks through the snow; there were only yours to be seen: and if you had had a little girl to go hand-in-hand with you up the hill, don't you think the foot-prints would have gone along with yours?'

'I can't help it, dear, dear Hester,' said she, crying, 'if they did not; I never looked at her feet, but she held my hand fast and tight in her little one, and it was very, very cold. She took me up the Fell path, up to the holly trees; and there I saw a lady weeping and crying; but when she saw me, she hushed her weeping, and smiled very proud and grand, and took me on her knee, and began to lull me to sleep; and that's all, Hester – but that is true; and my dear mamma knows it is,' said she, crying. So I thought the child was in a fever, and pretended to believe her, as she went over her story – over and over again, and always the same. At last Dorothy knocked at the door with Miss Rosamond's breakfast; and she told me the old ladies were down in the eating parlour, and that they wanted to speak to me. They had both been into the night-nursery the evening before, but it was after

Miss Rosamond was asleep; so they had only looked at her – not asked me any questions.

'I shall catch it,' thought I to myself, as I went along the north gallery. 'And yet,' I thought, taking courage, 'it was in their charge I left her; and it's they that's to blame for letting her steal away unknown and unwatched.' So I went in boldly, and told my story. I told it all to Miss Furnivall, shouting it close to her ear; but when I came to the mention of the other little girl out in the snow, coaxing and tempting her out, and willing her up to the grand and beautiful lady by the holly-tree, she threw her arms up – her old and withered arms – and cried aloud, 'Oh! Heaven, forgive! Have mercy!'

Mrs Stark took hold of her; roughly enough, I thought; but she was past Mrs Stark's management, and spoke to me, in a kind of wild warning and authority.

'Hester! keep her from that child! It will lure her to her death! That evil child! Tell her it is a wicked, naughty child.' Then, Mrs Stark hurried me out of the room; where, indeed, I was glad enough to go; but Miss Furnivall kept shrieking out, 'Oh! have mercy! Wilt Thou never forgive! It is many a long year ago –'

I was very uneasy in my mind after that. I durst never leave Miss Rosamond, night or day, for fear lest she might slip off again, after some fancy or other; and all the more, because I thought I could make out that Miss Furnivall was crazy, from their odd ways about her; and I was afraid lest something of the same kind (which might be in the family, you know) hung over my darling. And the great frost never ceased all this time; and, whenever it was a more stormy night than usual, between the gusts, and through the wind, we heard the old lord playing on the great organ. But, old lord, or not, wherever Miss Rosamond went, there I followed; for my love for her, pretty helpless orphan, was stronger than my fear for the grand and terrible sound. Besides, it rested with me to keep her cheerful and merry, as beseemed her age. So we played together, and wandered together, here and there, and everywhere; for I never dared to lose sight of her again in that large and rambling house, And so it happened, that one afternoon, not long before Christmas day, we were playing together on the billiard-table in the great hall (not that we knew the right way of playing, but she liked to roll the smooth ivory balls with her pretty hands, and I liked to do whatever she did); and, by-and-by, without our noticing it, it grew dusk indoors, though it was still light in the open air, and I was thinking of taking her back into the nursery, when, all of a sudden, she cried out:

'Look, Hester! look! there is my poor little girl out in the snow!'

I turned towards the long narrow windows, and there, sure enough, I saw a little girl, less than my Miss Rosamond – dressed all unfit to be out-of-doors such a bitter night – crying, and beating against the window-panes, as if she wanted to be let in. She seemed to sob and wail, till Miss Rosamond could bear it no longer, and was flying to the door to open it, when, all of a sudden, and close upon us, the great organ pealed out so loud and thundering, it fairly made me tremble; and all the more, when I remembered me that, even in the stillness of that dead-cold weather, I had heard no sound of little battering hands upon the window-glass, although the Phantom Child had seemed to put forth all its force; and, although I had seen it wail and cry, no faintest touch of sound had fallen upon my ears. Whether I remembered all this at the very moment, I do not know; the great organ sound had so stunned me into terror; but this I know, I caught up Miss Rosamond before she got the hall-door opened, and clutched her, and carried her away, kicking and screaming, into the large bright kitchen, where Dorothy and Agnes were busy with their mince-pies.

'What is the matter with my sweet one?' cried Dorothy, as I bore in Miss Rosamond, who was sobbing as if her heart would break.

'She won't let me open the door for my little girl to come in; and she'll die if she is out on the Fells all night. Cruel, naughty Hester,' she said, slapping me; but she might have struck harder, for I had seen a look of ghastly terror on

Dorothy's face, which made my very blood run cold.

'Shut the back kitchen door fast, and bolt it well,' said she to Agnes. She said no more; she gave me raisins and almonds to quiet Miss Rosamond: but she sobbed about the little girl in the snow, and would not touch any of the good things. I was thankful when she cried herself to sleep in bed. Then I stole down to the kitchen, and told Dorothy I had made up my mind. I would carry my darling back to my father's house in Applethwaite; where, if we lived humbly, we lived at peace. I said I had been frightened enough with the old lord's organ-playing; but now, that I had seen for myself this little moaning child, all decked out as no child in the neighbourhood could be, beating and battering to get in, yet always without any sound or noise – with the dark wound on its right shoulder; and that Miss Rosamond had known it again for the phantom that had nearly lured her to her death (which Dorothy knew was true); I would stand it no longer.

I saw Dorothy change colour once or twice. When I had done, she told me she did not think I could take Miss Rosamond with me, for that she was my lord's ward, and I had no right over her; and she asked me, would I leave the child that I was so fond of, just for sounds and sights that could do me no harm; and that they had all had to get used to in their turns? I was all in a hot, trembling passion; and I said it was very well for her to talk, that knew what these sights and noises betokened, and that had, perhaps, had something to do with the Spectre-Child while it was alive. And I taunted her so, that she told me all she knew, at last; and then I wished I had never been told, for it only made me more afraid than ever.

She said she had heard the tale from old neighbours, that were alive when she was first married; when folks used to come to the hall sometimes, before it had got such a bad name on the country side: it might not be true, or it might, what she had been told.

The old lord was Miss Furnivall's father – Miss Grace, as Dorothy called her, for Miss Maude was the elder, and Miss Furnivall by rights. The old lord was eaten up with pride.

Such a proud man was never seen or heard of; and his daughters were like him. No one was good enough to wed them, although they had choice enough; for they were the great beauties of their day, as I had seen by their portraits, where they hung in the state drawing-room. But, as the old saying is, 'Pride will have a fall'; and these two haughty beauties fell in love with the same man, and he no better than a foreign musician, whom their father had down from London to play music with him at the Manor House. For, above all things, next to his pride, the old lord loved music. He could play on nearly every instrument that ever was heard of: and it was a strange thing it did not soften him; but he was a fierce dour old man, and had broken his poor wife's heart with his cruelty, they said. He was mad after music, and would pay any money for it. So he got this foreigner to come; who made such beautiful music, that they said the very birds on the trees stopped their singing to listen. And, by degrees, this foreign gentleman got such a hold over the old lord, that nothing would serve him but that he must come every year; and it was he that had the great organ brought from Holland, and built up in the hall, where it stood now. He taught the old lord to play on it; but many and many a time, when Lord Furnivall was thinking of nothing but his fine organ, and his finer music, the dark foreigner was walking abroad in the woods with one of the young ladies; now Miss Maude, and then Miss Grace.

Miss Maude won the day and carried off the prize, such as it was; and he and she were married, all unknown to any one; and before he made his next yearly visit, she had been confined of a little girl at a farm-house on the Moors, while her father and Miss Grace thought she was away at Doncaster Races. But though she was a wife and a mother, she was not a bit softened, but was haughty and as passionate as ever; and perhaps more so, for she was jealous of Miss Grace, to whom her foreign husband paid a deal of court – by way of blinding her – as he told his wife. But Miss Grace triumphed over Miss Maude, and Miss Maude grew fiercer and fiercer, both with her husband and with her sister; and the former – who could easily shake off what was disagreeable, and hide himself in foreign countries – went away a month before his usual time that summer, and half-threatened that he would never come back again. Meanwhile, the little girl was left at the farm-house, and her mother used to have her horse saddled and gallop wildly over the hills to see her once every week, at the very least – for where she loved, she loved; and where she hated, she hated. And the old lord went on playing – playing on his organ; and the servants thought the sweet music he made had soothed down his awful temper, of which (Dorothy said) some terrible tales could be told. He grew infirm too, and had to walk with a crutch; and his son – that was the present Lord Furnivall's father – was with the army in America, and the other son at sea; so Miss Maude had it pretty much her own way, and she and Miss Grace grew colder and bitterer to each other every day; till at last they hardly ever spoke, except when the old lord was by. The foreign musician came again the next summer, but it was for the last time; for they led him such a life with their jealousy and their passions, that he grew weary, and went away, and never was heard of again. And Miss Maude, who had always meant to have her marriage acknowledged when her father should be dead, was left now a deserted wife – whom nobody knew to have been married – with a child that she dared not own, although she loved it to distraction; living with a father whom she feared, and a sister whom she hated. When the next summer passed over and the dark foreigner never came, both Miss Maude and Miss Grace grew gloomy and sad; they had a haggard look about them, though they looked handsome as ever. But by-and-by Miss Maude brightened; for her father grew more and more infirm, and more than ever carried away by his music; and she and Miss Grace lived almost entirely apart, having separate rooms, the one on the west side, Miss Maude on the east – those very rooms which were now shut up. So she thought she might have her little girl with her, and no one need ever know except those who dared not speak about it, and were bound to believe that it was, as she said, a cottager's child she had taken a fancy to. All this, Dorothy said, was pretty well known; but what came afterwards no one knew, except Miss Grace, and Mrs Stark, who was even then her maid, and much more of a friend to her than ever her sister had been. But the servants supposed, from words that were dropped, that Miss Maude had triumphed over Miss Grace, and told her that all the time the dark foreigner had been mocking her with pretended love – he was her own husband; the colour left Miss Grace's cheek and lips that very day for ever, and she was heard to say many a time that sooner or later she would have her revenge; and Mrs Stark was for ever spying about the east rooms.

One fearful night, just after the New Year had come in, when the snow was lying thick and deep, and the flakes were still falling – fast enough to blind any one who might be out and abroad – there was a great and violent noise heard, and the old lord's voice above all, cursing and swearing awfully, – and the cries of a little child, – and the proud defiance of a fierce woman, – and the sound of a blow, – and a dead stillness, – and moans and wailings dying away on the hill-side! Then the old lord summoned all his servants, and told them, with terrible oaths, and words more terrible, that his daughter had disgraced herself, and that he had turned her out of doors, – her, and her child, – and that if ever they gave her help, – or food – or shelter, – he prayed that they might never enter Heaven. And, all the while, Miss Grace stood by him, white and still as any stone; and when he had ended she heaved a great sigh, as much as to say her work was done, and her end was accomplished. But the old lord never touched his organ again, and died within the year; and no wonder! for, on the morrow of that wild and fearful night, the shepherds, coming down the Fell side, found Miss Maude sitting, all crazy and smiling, under the holly-trees, nursing a dead child, – with a terrible mark on its right shoulder. 'But that was not what killed it,' said Dorothy; 'it was the frost and the cold; – every wild creature was in its hole, and every beast in its fold, – while the child and its mother were turned out to wander on the Fells! And now you know all! and I wonder if you are less frightened now?'

I was more frightened than ever; but I said I was not. I wished Miss Rosamond and myself well out of that dreadful house for ever; but I would not leave her, and I dared not take her away. But oh! how I watched her, and guarded her! We bolted the doors, and shut the window-shutters fast, an hour or more before dark, rather than leave them open five minutes too late. But my little lady still heard the weird child crying and mourning; and not all we could do or say, could keep her from wanting to go to her, and let her in from the cruel wind and the snow. All this time, I kept away from Miss Furnivall and Mrs Stark, as much as ever I could; for I feared them – I knew no good could be about them, with their grey hard faces, and their dreamy eyes, looking back into the ghastly years that were gone. But, even in my fear, I had a kind of pity – for Miss Furnivall, at least. Those gone down to the pit can hardly have a more hopeless look than that which was ever on her face. At last I even got so sorry for her – who never said a word but what was quite forced from her – that I prayed for her; and I taught Miss Rosamond to pray for one who had done a deadly sin; but often when she came to those words, she would listen, and start up from her knees, and say, 'I hear my little girl plaining and crying very sad – Oh! let her in, or she will die!'

One night – just after New Year's Day had come at last, and the long winter had taken a turn, as I hoped – I heard the west drawing-room bell ring three times, which was the signal for me. I would not leave Miss Rosamond alone, for all she was asleep – for the old lord had been playing wilder than ever – and I feared lest my darling should waken to hear the spectre child; see her I knew she could not. I had fastened the windows too well for that. So, I took her out of her bed and wrapped her up in such outer clothes as were most handy, and carried her down to the drawing-room, where the old ladies sat at their tapestry work as usual. They looked up when I came in, and Mrs Stark asked, quite astounded, 'Why did I bring Miss Rosamond there, out of her warm bed?' I had begun to whisper, 'Because I was afraid of her being tempted out while I was away, by the wild child in the snow,' when she stopped me short (with a glance at Miss Furnivall), and said Miss Furnivall wanted me to undo some work she had done wrong, and which neither of them could see to unpick. So, I laid my pretty dear on the sofa, and sat down on a stool by them, and hardened my heart against them, as I heard the wind rising and howling.

Miss Rosamond slept on sound, for all the wind blew so; and Miss Furnivall said never a word, nor looked round when the gusts shook the windows. All at once she started up to her full height, and put up one hand, as if to bid us listen.

'I hear voices!' said she. 'I hear terrible screams – I hear my father's voice!'

Just at that moment, my darling wakened with a sudden start: 'My little girl is crying, oh, how she is crying!' and she tried to get up and go to her, but she got her feet entangled in the blanket, and I caught her up; for my flesh had begun to creep at these noises, which they heard while we could catch no sound. In a minute or two the noises came, and gathered fast, and filled our ears; we, too, heard voices and screams, and no longer heard the winter's wind that raged abroad. Mrs Stark looked at me, and I at her, but we dared not speak. Suddenly Miss Furnivall went towards the door, out into the ante-room, through the west lobby, and opened the door into the great hall. Mrs Stark followed, and I durst not be left, though my heart almost stopped beating for fear. I wrapped my darling tight in my arms, and went out with them. In the hall the screams were louder than ever; they sounded to come from the east wing – nearer and nearer – close on the other side of the locked-up doors – close behind them. Then I noticed that the great bronze chandelier seemed all alight, though the hall was dim, and that a fire was blazing in the vast hearth-place, though it gave no heat; and I shuddered up with terror, and folded my darling closer to me. But as I did so, the east door shook, and she, suddenly struggling to get free from me, cried, 'Hester! I must go! My little girl is there; I hear her; she is coming! Hester, I must go!'

I held her tight with all my strength; with a set will, I held her. If I had died, my hands would have grasped her still, I was so resolved in my mind. Miss Furnivall stood listening, and paid no regard to my darling, who had got down to the ground, and whom I, upon my knees now, was holding with both my arms clasped round her neck; she still striving and crying to get free.

All at once, the east door gave way with a thundering crash, as if torn open in a violent passion, and there came into that broad and mysterious light, the figure of a tall old man, with grey hair and gleaming eyes. He drove before him, with many a relentless gesture of abhorrence, a stern and beautiful woman, with a little child clinging to her dress.

'Oh Hester! Hester!' cried Miss Rosamond. 'It's the lady! the lady below the holly-trees; and my little girl is with her. Hester! Hester! let me go to her; they are drawing me to them. I feel them – I feel them. I must go!'

Again she was almost convulsed by her efforts to get away; but I held her tighter and tighter, till I feared I should do her a hurt; but rather that than let her go towards those terrible phantoms. They passed along towards the great hall-door, where the winds howled and ravened for their prey; but before they reached that, the lady turned; and I could see that she defied the old man with a fierce and proud defiance; but then she quailed – and then she threw up her arms wildly and piteously to save her child – her little child – from a blow from his uplifted crutch.

And Miss Rosamond was torn as by a power stronger than mine, and writhed in my arms, and sobbed (for by this time the poor darling was growing faint).

'They want me to go with them on to the Fells – they are drawing me to them. Oh, my little girl! I would come, but cruel, wicked Hester holds me very tight.' But when she saw the uplifted crutch she swooned away, and I thanked God for it. Just at this moment – when the tall old man, his hair streaming as in the blast of a furnace, was going to strike the little shrinking child – Miss Furnivall, the old woman by my side, cried out, 'Oh, father! father! spare the little innocent child!' But just then I saw – we all saw – another phantom shape itself, and grow clear out of the blue and misty light that filled the hall; we had not seen her till now, for it was another lady who stood by the old man, with a look of relentless hate and triumphant scorn. That figure was very beautiful to look upon, with a soft white hat drawn down over the proud brows, and a red and curling lip. It was dressed in an open robe of blue satin. I had seen that figure before. It was the likeness of Miss Furnivall in her youth; and the terrible phantoms moved on, regardless of old Miss Furnivall's wild entreaty, – and the uplifted crutch fell on the right shoulder of the little child, and the younger sister looked on, stony and deadly serene. But at that moment, the dim lights, and the fire that gave no heat, went out of themselves, and Miss Furnivall lay at our feet stricken down by the palsy – death-stricken.

Yes! she was carried to her bed that night never to rise again. She lay with her face to the wall, muttering low but muttering alway: 'Alas! alas! what is done in youth can never be undone in age! What is done in youth can never be undone in age!'

The Signalman

by Charles Dickens

More words have probably been written about Charles Dickens (1812–1870) than are contained in all his books put together and little else can be added. However, it might be fair to say that Dickens' own liking for the macabre has generally been understated. As a boy he was addicted to penny dreadfuls and he later admitted 'making myself unspeakably miserable and frightening my very wits out of my head for the small charge of a penny weekly which, considering that there was an illustration to every number in which there was always a pool of blood, and at least one body, was cheap'. It would be ironic if the best-loved of all Victorian writers had been inspired to take up writing by the perusal of such much-disdained fare!

Dickens' contribution to supernatural literature was not limited to such well-known stories as The Trial for Murder; A Christmas Carol; The Chimes *and* The Haunted Man and the Ghost's Bargain. *As editor of the immensely popular magazine* Household Words *(later* All the Year Round, *after a quarrel with the publishers) he was able to encourage the writing and publication of such stories. In particular, the Christmas numbers of these periodicals contained some of the finest ghost stories ever written. Dickens' own ghost stories tend towards a moralising attitude – perhaps an influence of his mentor Leigh Hunt who wrote that a good ghost story should add to the 'utility of excitement a moral utility.' Fortunately,* The Signalman *offers only terror, pure and undiluted.*

'HALLOA! Below there!'

When he heard a voice thus calling to him, he was standing at the door of his box, with a flag in his hand, furled round its short pole. One would have thought, considering the nature of the ground, that he could not have doubted from what quarter the voice came; but, instead of looking up to where I stood on the top of the steep cutting nearly over his head, he turned himself about and looked down the Line. There was something remarkable in his manner of doing so, though I could not have said, for my life, what. But, I know it was remarkable enough to attract my notice, even though his figure was foreshortened and shadowed, down in the deep trench, and mine was high above him, so steeped in the glow of an angry sunset that I had shaded my eyes with my hand before I saw him at all.

'Halloa! Below!'

From looking down the Line, he turned himself about again, and, raising his eyes, saw my figure high above him.

'Is there any path by which I can come down and speak to you?'

He looked up at me without replying, and I looked down at him without pressing him too soon with a repetition of my idle question. Just then, there came a vague vibration in the earth and air, quickly changing into a violent pulsation, and an oncoming rush that caused me to start back, as though it had force to draw me down. When such vapour as rose to my height from the said train, had passed me and was skimming away over the landscape, I looked down again, and saw him re-furling the flag he had shown while the train went by.

I repeated my inquiry. After a pause, during which he seemed to regard me with fixed attention, he motioned with his rolled-up flag towards a point on my level, some two or three hundred yards distant. I called down to him, 'All right!' and made for that point. There, by dint of looking closely about me, I found a rough zig-zag descending path notched out: which I followed.

The cutting was extremely deep, and unusually precipitate. It was made through a clammy stone that became oozier and wetter as I went down. For these reasons, I found the way long enough to give me time to recall a singular air of reluctance or compulsion with which he had pointed out the path.

When I came down low enough upon the zig-zag descent, to see him again, I saw that he was standing between the rails on the way, by which the train had lately passed, in an attitude as if he were waiting for me to appear. He had his left hand at his chin, and that left elbow rested on his right hand crossed over his breast. His attitude was one of such expectation and watchfulness, that I stopped a moment, wondering at it.

I resumed my downward way, and, stepping out upon the level of the railroad and drawing nearer to him, saw that he was a dark sallow man, with a dark beard and rather heavy eyebrows. His post was in as solitary and dismal a place as ever I saw. On either side, a dripping-wet wall of jagged stone, excluding all view but a strip of sky; the perspective one way, only a crooked prolongation of this great dungeon; the shorter perspective in the other direction, terminating in a gloomy red light, and the gloomier entrance to a black tunnel, in whose massive architecture there was a barbarous, depressing, and forbidding air. So little sunlight ever found its way to this spot, that it had an earthy deadly smell; and so much cold wind rushed through it, that it struck chill to me, as if I had left the natural world.

Before he stirred, I was near enough to him to have touched him. Not even then removing his eyes from mine, he stepped back one step, and lifted his hand.

This was a lonesome post to occupy (I said), and it had riveted my attention when I looked down from up yonder. A visitor was a rarity, I should suppose; not an unwelcome rarity, I hoped? In me, he merely saw a man who had been shut up within narrow limits all his life, and who, being at last set free, had a newly-awakened interest in these great works. To such purpose I spoke to him; but I am far from sure of the terms I used, for, besides that I am not happy in opening any conversation, there was something in the man that daunted me.

He directed a most curious look towards the red light near the tunnel's mouth, and looked all about it, as if something were missing from it, and then looked at me.

That light was part of his charge? Was it not?

He answered in a low voice: 'Don't you know it is?'

The monstrous thought came into my mind as I perused the fixed eyes and the saturnine face, that this was a spirit, not a man. I have speculated since, whether there may have been infection in his mind.

In my turn, I stepped back. But in making the action, I detected in his eyes some latent fear of me. This put the monstrous thought to flight.

'You look at me,' I said, forcing a smile, 'as if you had a dread of me.'

'I was doubtful,' he returned, 'whether I had seen you before.'

'Where?'

He pointed to the red light he had looked at.

'There?' I said.

Intently watchful of me, he replied (but without sound), Yes.

'My good fellow, what should I do there? However, be that as it may, I never was there, you may swear.'

'I think I may,' he rejoined. 'Yes. I am sure I may.'

His manner cleared, like my own. He replied to my remarks with readiness, and in well-chosen words. Had he much to do there? Yes; that was to say, he had enough responsibility to bear; but exactness and watchfulness were what was required of him, and of actual work – manual labour – he had next to none. To change that signal, to trim those lights, and to turn this iron handle now and then, was all he had to do under that head. Regarding those many long and lonely hours of which I seemed to make so much, he could only say that the routine of his life had shaped itself into that form, and he had grown used to it. He had taught himself a language down here – if only to know it by sight, and to have formed his own crude ideas of its pronunciation, could be called learning it. He had also worked at fractions and decimals and tried a little algebra; but he was, and had been as a boy, a poor hand at figures. Was it necessary for him when on duty , always to remain in that channel of damp air, and could he never rise into the sunshine from between those high stone walls? Why, that depended upon times and circumstances. Under some conditions there would be less upon the Line than under others, and the same held good as to certain hours of the day and night. In bright weather, he did choose occasions for getting a little above these lower shadows; but, being at all times liable to be called by his electric bell, and at such times listening for it with redoubled anxiety, the relief was less than I would suppose.

He took me into his box, where there was a fire, a desk for an official book in which he had to make certain entries, a telegraphic instrument with its dial face and needles, and the little bell of which he had spoken. On my trusting that he would excuse the remark that he had been well educated, and (I hoped I might say without offence), perhaps educated above that station, he observed that instances of slight incongruity in such-wise would rarely be found wanting among large bodies of men; that he had heard it was so in workhouses, in the police force, even in that last desperate resource, the army; and that he knew it was so, more or less, in any great railway staff. He had been, when young (if I could believe it, sitting in that hut; he scarcely could), a student of natural philosophy, and had attended lectures; but he had run wild, misused his opportunities, gone down, and never risen again. He had no complaint to offer about that. He had made his bed, and he lay upon it. It was far too late to make another.

All that I have here condensed, he said in a quiet manner, with his grave dark regards divided between me and the fire. He threw in the word 'Sir', from time to time, and especially when he referred to his youth: as though to request me to understand that he claimed to be nothing but what I found him. He was several times interrupted by the little bell, and had to read off messages, and send replies. Once, he had to stand without the door, and display a flag as a train passed, and make some verbal communication to the driver. In the discharge of his duties I observed him to be remarkably exact and vigilant, breaking off his discourse at a syllable, and remaining silent until what he had to do was done.

In a word, I should have set this man down as one of the safest of men to be employed in that capacity, but for the circumstance that while he was speaking to me he twice broke off with a fallen colour, turned his face towards the little bell when it did NOT ring, opened the door of the hut (which was kept shut to exclude the unhealthy damp), and looked out towards the red light near the mouth of the tunnel. On both of those occasions, he came back to the fire with the inexplicable air upon him which I had remarked, without being able to define, when we were so far asunder.

Said I when I rose to leave him: 'You almost make me think that I have met with a contented man.'

(I am afraid I must acknowledge that I said it to lead him on.)

'I believe I used to be so,' he rejoined, in the low voice in which he had first spoken; 'but I am troubled, sir, I am troubled.'

He would have recalled the words if he could. He had said them, however, and I took them up quickly.

'With what? What is your trouble?'

'It is very difficult to impart, sir. It is very, very, difficult to speak of. If ever you make me another visit, I will try to tell you.'

'But I expressly intend to make you another visit. Say, when shall it be?'

'I go off early in the morning, and I shall be on again at ten tomorrow night, sir.'

'I will come at eleven.'

He thanked me, and went out at the door with me. 'I'll show my white light, sir,' he said, in his peculiar low voice, 'till you have found the way up. When you have found it, don't call out! And when you are at the top, don't call out!'

His manner seemed to make the place strike colder to me, but I said no more than 'Very well.'

'And when you come down tomorrow night, don't call out! Let me ask you a parting question. What made you cry "Halloa! Below there!" tonight?'

'Heaven knows,' said I. 'I cried something to that effect – '

'Not to that effect, sir. Those were the very words. I know them well.'

'Admit those were the very words. I said them, no doubt, because I saw you below.'

'For no other reason?'

'What other reason could I possibly have?'

'You had no feeling that they were conveyed to you in any supernatural way?'

'No.'

He wished me good night, and held up his light. I walked by the side of the down Line of rails (with a very disagreeable sensation of a train coming behind me), until I found the path. It was easier to mount than to descend, and I got back to my inn without any adventure.

Punctual to my appointment, I placed my foot on the first notch of the zig-zag next night, as the distant clocks were striking eleven. He was waiting for me at the bottom, with his white light on. 'I have not called out,' I said, when we came close together; 'may I speak now?' 'By all means, sir.' 'Good night then, and here's my hand.' 'Good night, sir, and here's mine.' With that, we walked side by side to his box, entered it, closed the door, and sat down by the fire.

'I have made up my mind, sir,' he began, bending forward as soon as we were seated, and speaking in a tone but a little above a whisper, 'that you shall not have to ask me twice what troubles me. I took you for some one else yesterday evening. That troubles me.'

'That mistake?'

'No. That some one else.'

'Who is it?'

'I don't know.'

'Like me?'

'I don't know. I never saw the face. The left arm is across the face and the right arm is waved. Violently waved. This way.'

I followed his action with my eyes, and it was the action of an arm gesticulating with the utmost passion and vehemence: 'For God's sake clear the way!'

'One moonlight night,' said the man, 'I was sitting here, when I heard a voice cry "Halloa! Below there!" I started up, looked from that door, and saw this Some one else standing by the red light near the tunnel, waving as I just now showed you. The voice seemed hoarse with shouting, and it cried, "Look out! Look out!" And then again "Halloa! Below there! Look out!" I caught up my lamp, turned it on red, and ran towards the figure calling, "What's wrong? What has happened? Where?" It stood just outside the blackness of the tunnel. I advanced so close upon it that I wondered at its keeping the sleeve across its eyes. I ran right up at it, and had my hand stretched out to pull the sleeve away, when it was gone.'

'Into the tunnel,' said I.

'No. I ran on into the tunnel, five hundred yards. I stopped and held my lamp above my head and saw the figures of the measured distance, and saw the wet stains stealing down the walls and trickling through the arch. I ran out again, faster than I had run in (for I had a mortal abhorrence of the place upon me), and I looked all round the red light with my own red light, and I went up the iron ladder to the gallery atop of it, and I came down again, and ran back here. I telegraphed both ways: "An alarm has been given. Is anything wrong?" The answer came back, both ways: "All well." '

Resisting the slow touch of a frozen finger tracing out my spine, I showed him how that this figure must be a deception of his sense of sight, and how that figures, originating in disease of the delicate nerves that minister to the functions of the eye, were known to have often troubled patients, some of whom had become conscious of the nature of their affliction, and had even proved it by experiments upon themselves. 'As to an imaginary cry,' said I, 'do but listen for a moment to the wind in this unnatural valley while we speak so low, and to the wild harp it makes of the telegraph wires?'

That was all very well, he returned, after we had sat listening for a while, and he ought to know something of the wind and the wires, he who so often passed long winter nights there, alone and watching. But he would beg to remark that he had not finished.

I asked his pardon, and he slowly added these words, touching my arm:

'Within six hours after the Appearance, the memorable accident on this Line happened, and within ten hours the dead and wounded were brought along through the tunnel over the spot where the figure had stood.'

A disagreeable shudder crept over me, but I did my best against it. It was not to be denied, I rejoined, that this was a remarkable coincidence, calculated deeply to impress his mind. But, it was unquestionable that remarkable coincidences did continually occur, and they must be taken into account in dealing with such a subject. Though to be sure I must admit, I added (for I thought I saw that he was going to bring the objection to bear upon me), men of common sense did not allow much for coincidences in making the ordinary calculations of life.

He again begged to remark that he had not finished.

I again begged his pardon for being betrayed into interruptions.

'This,' he said, again laying his hand upon my arm, and glancing over his shoulder with hollow eyes, 'was just a year ago. Six or seven months passed, and I had recovered from the surprise and shock, when one morning, as the day was breaking, I, standing at that door, looked towards the red light, and saw the spectre again.' He stopped, with a fixed look at me.

'Did it cry out?'

'No. It was silent.'

'Did it wave its arm?'

'No. It leaned against the shaft of the light, with both hands before the face. Like this.'

Once more, I followed his action with my eyes. It was an action of mourning. I have seen such an attitude in stone figures on tombs.

'Did you go up to it?'

'I came in and sat down, partly to collect my thoughts, partly because it had turned me faint. When I went to the door again, daylight was above me, and the ghost was gone.'

'But nothing followed? Nothing came of this?'

He touched me on the arm with his forefinger twice or thrice, giving a ghastly nod each time:

'That very day, as a train came out of the tunnel, I noticed at a carriage window on my side, what looked like a confusion of hands and heads, and something waved. I saw it, just in time to signal the driver, Stop! He shut off, and put his brake on, but the train drifted past here a hundred and fifty yards or more. I ran after it, and, as I went along, heard terrible screams and cries. A beautiful young lady had died instantaneously in one of the compartments, and was brought in here, and laid down on this floor between us.'

Involuntarily, I pushed my chair back, as I looked from the boards at which he pointed, to himself.

'True, sir. True. Precisely as it happened, so I tell it you.'

I could think of nothing to say, to any purpose, and my mouth was very dry. The wind and the wires took up the story with a long lamenting wail.

He resumed. 'Now, sir, mark this, and judge how my mind is troubled. The spectre came back, a week ago. Ever since, it has been there, now and again, by fits and starts.'

'At the light?'

'At the Danger-light.'

'What does it seem to do?'

He repeated, if possible with increased passion and vehemence, that former gesticulation of 'For God's sake clear the way!'

Then, he went on. 'I have no peace or rest for it. It calls to me, for many minutes together, in an agonised manner,

"Below there! Look out! Look out!" It stands waving to me. It rings my little bell – '

I caught at that. 'Did it ring your bell yesterday evening when I was here, and you went to the door?'

'Twice.'

'Why, see,' said I, 'how your imagination misleads you. My eyes were on the bell, and my ears were open to the bell, and if I am a living man, it did NOT ring at those times. No, nor at any other time, except when it was rung in the natural course of physical things by the station communicating with you.'

He shook his head. 'I have never made a mistake as to that, yet, sir. I have never confused the spectre's ring with the man's. The ghost's ring is a strange vibration in the bell that it derives from nothing else, and I have not asserted that the bell stirs to the eye. I don't wonder that you failed to hear it. But *I* heard it.'

'And did the spectre seem to be there, when you looked out?'

'It WAS there.'

'Both times?'

He repeated firmly: 'Both times.'

'Will you come to the door with me, and look for it now?'

He bit his under-lip as though he were somewhat unwilling, but arose. I opened the door, and stood on the step, while he stood in the doorway. There, was the Danger-light. There, was the dismal mouth of the tunnel. There, were the high wet stone walls of the cutting. There, were the stars above them.

'Do you see it?' I asked him, taking particular note of his face. His eyes were prominent and strained; but not very much more so, perhaps, than my own had been when I had directed them earnestly towards the same spot.

'No,' he answered. 'It is not there.'

'Agreed,' said I.

We went in again, shut the door, and resumed our seats. I was thinking how best to improve this advantage, if it might be called one, when he took up the conversation in such a matter of course way, so assuming that there could be no serious question of fact between us, that I felt myself placed in the weakest of positions.

'By this time you will fully understand, sir,' he said, 'that what troubles me so dreadfully, is the question, What does the spectre mean?'

I was not sure, I told him, that I did fully understand.

'What is its warning against?' he said, ruminating, with his eyes on the fire, and only by times turning them on me. 'What is the danger? Where is the danger? There is danger overhanging, somewhere on the Line. Some dreadful calamity will happen. It is not to be doubted this third time, after what has gone before. But surely this is a cruel haunting of *me*. What can *I* do?'

He pulled out his handkerchief, and wiped the drops from his heated forehead.

'If I telegraph Danger, on either side of me, or on both, I can give no reason for it,' he went on, wiping the palms of his hands. 'I should get into trouble, and do no good. They would think I was mad. This is the way it would work: – Message: "Danger! Take care!" Answer: "What Danger? Where?" Message: "Don't know. But for God's sake take care!" They would displace me. What else could they do?'

His pain of mind was most pitiable to see. It was the mental torture of a conscientious man, oppressed beyond endurance by unintelligible responsibility involving life.

'When it first stood under the Danger-light,' he went on, putting his dark hair back from his head, and drawing his hands outward across and across his temples in an extremity of feverish distress, 'why not tell me where that accident was to happen – if it must happen? Why not tell me how it could be averted – if it could have been averted? When on its second coming it hid its face, why not tell me instead: "She is going to die. Let them keep her at home"? If it came, on those two occasions, only to show me that its warnings were true, and so to prepare me for the third, why not warn me plainly now? And I, Lord help me! A mere poor signalman on this solitary station! Why not go to somebody with credit to be believed, and power to act!'

When I saw him in this state, I saw that for the poor man's sake, as well as for the public safety, what I had to do for the time was, to compose his mind. Therefore, setting aside all question of reality or unreality between us, I represented to him that whoever thoroughly discharged his duty, must do well, and that at least it was his comfort that he understood his duty, though he did not understand these confounding Appearances. In this effort I succeeded far better than in the attempt to reason him out of his conviction. He became calm; the occupations incidental to his post as the night advanced, began to make larger demands on his attention; and I left him at two in the morning. I had offered to stay through the night, but he would not hear of it.

That I more than once looked back at the red light as I ascended the pathway, that I did not like the red light, and that I should have slept but poorly if my bed had been under it, I see no reason to conceal. Nor, did I like the two sequences of the accident and the dead girl. I see no reason to conceal that, either.

But, what ran most in my thoughts was the consideration how ought I to act, having become the recipient of this disclosure? I had proved the man to be intelligent, vigilant, painstaking, and exact; but how long might he remain so, in his state of mind? Though in a subordinate position, still he held a most important trust, and would I (for instance) like to stake my own life on the chances of his continuing to execute it with precision?

Unable to overcome a feeling that there would be something treacherous in my communicating what he had told me, to his superiors in the Company, without first being plain with himself and proposing a middle course to him, I ultimately resolved to offer to accompany him (otherwise keeping his secret for the present) to the wisest medical practitioner we could hear of in those parts, and to take his opinion. A change in his time of duty would come round next night, he had apprised me, and he would be off an hour or two after sunrise, and on again soon after sunset. I had appointed to return accordingly.

Next evening was a lovely evening, and I walked out early to enjoy it. The sun was not yet quite down when I traversed the field-path near the top of the deep cutting. I would extend my walk for an hour, I said to myself, half an hour on and half an hour back, and it would then be time to go to my signalman's box.

Before pursuing my stroll, I stepped to the brink, and mechanically looked down, from the point from which I had first seen him. I cannot describe the thrill that seized upon me, when, close at the mouth of the tunnel, I saw the appearance of a man, with his left sleeve across his eyes, passionately waving his right arm.

The nameless horror that oppressed me, passed in a moment, for in a moment I saw that this appearance of a man was a man indeed, and that there was a little group of other men standing at a short distance, to whom he seemed to be rehearsing the gesture he made. The Danger-light was not yet lighted. Against its shaft, a little low hut, entirely new to me, had been made of some wooden supports and tarpaulin. It looked no bigger than a bed.

With an irresistible sense that something was wrong – with a flashing self-reproachful fear that fatal mischief had come of my leaving the man there, and causing no one to be sent to overlook or correct what he did – I descended the notched path with all the speed I could make.

'What is the matter?' I asked the men.

'Signalman killed this morning, sir.'

'Not the man belonging to that box?'

'Yes, sir.'

'Not the man I know?'

'You will recognise him, sir, if you knew him,' said the man who spoke for the others, solemnly uncovering his own head and raising an end of the tarpaulin, 'for his face is quite composed.'

'Oh! how did this happen, how did this happen?' I asked, turning from one to another as the hut closed in again.

'He was cut down by an engine, sir. No man in England knew his work better. But somehow he was not clear of the outer rail. It was just at broad day. He had struck the light, and had the lamp in his hand. As the engine came out of the tunnel, his back was towards her, and she cut him down. That man drove her, and was showing how it happened. Show the gentleman, Tom.'

The man, who wore a rough dark dress, stepped back to his former place at the mouth of the tunnel:

'Coming round the curve in the tunnel, sir,' he said, 'I saw him at the end, like as if I saw him down a perspective-glass. There was no time to check speed, and I knew him to be very careful. As he didn't seem to take heed of the whistle, I shut it off when we were running down upon him, and called to him as loud as I could call.'

'What did you say?'

'I said, Below there! Look out! Look out! For God's sake clear the way!'

I started.

'Ah! it was a dreadful time, sir, I never left off calling to him. I put this arm before my eyes, not to see, and I waved this arm to the last; but it was no use.'

Without prolonging the narrative to dwell on any one of its curious circumstances more than on any other, I may, in closing it, point out the coincidence that the warning of the Engine-Driver included, not only the words which the unfortunate Signalman had repeated to me as haunting him, but also the words which I myself – not he – had attached, and that only in my own mind, to the gesticulation he had imitated.

THE END